She Was Caught in a Whirlwind of Emotion...

"I'll take care of you, Hannah. I'll make you happy. Just give yourself to me," Jarrett murmured against her lips.

His words poured over her like warm honey, sweet and tantalizing and full of masculine promise. Hannah shivered, fiercely aware of a wild, new recklessness moving within her.

On one level she was frightened of this man she scarcely knew, but on another she was inexplicably drawn to him. Now he had declared that he wanted her, her dreams, her wildest fantasies, were waiting to be fulfilled. All she had to do was surrender....

Dear Reader,

Welcome to Silhouette! Our goal is to give you hours of unbeatable reading pleasure, and we hope you'll enjoy each month's six new Silhouette Desires. These sensual, provocative love stories are both believable and compelling—sometimes they're poignant, sometimes humorous, but always enjoyable.

Indulge yourself. Experience all the passion and excitement of falling in love along with our heroine as she meets the irresistible man of her dreams and together they overcome all obstacles in the path to a happy ending.

If this is your first Desire, I hope it'll be the first of many. If you're already a Silhouette Desire reader, thanks for your support! Look for some of your favorite authors in the coming months: Stephanie James, Diana Palmer, Dixie Browning, Ann Major and Doreen Owens Malek, to name just a few.

Happy reading!

Isabel Swift
Senior Editor

STEPHANIE JAMES
Golden Goddess

Silhouette Desire

Published by Silhouette Books New York

America's Publisher of Contemporary Romance

SILHOUETTE BOOKS
300 E. 42nd St., New York, N.Y. 10017

Copyright © 1985 by Jayne Krentz Inc.

Distributed by Pocket Books

ISBN 0-373-05235-9

First Silhouette Books printing October 1985

10 9 8 7 6 5 4 3 2 1

America's Publisher of Contemporary Romance

Printed in the U.S.A.

Books by Stephanie James

Silhouette Desire

Corporate Affair #1
Velvet Touch #11
Lover in Pursuit #19
Renaissance Man #25
Reckless Passion #31
Price of Surrender #37
Affair of Honor #49
To Tame the Hunter #55
Gamemaster #67
The Silver Snare #85
Battle Prize #97
Body Guard #103
Gambler's Woman #115
Fabulous Beast #127
Night of the Magician #145
Nightwalker #163
The Devil to Pay #187
Wizard #211
Golden Goddess #235

Silhouette Intimate Moments

Serpent in Paradise #9
Raven's Prey #21

STEPHANIE JAMES

readily admits that the chief influence on her writing is her "lifelong addiction to romantic daydreaming." She has spent the past nine years living and working with her engineer husband in a wide variety of places, including the Caribbean, the Southeast and the Pacific Northwest. Ms. James currently resides in Washington. Stephanie James is a pseudonym for Jayne Krentz, who also writes as Jayne Castle.

One

By the time Hannah Prescott realized there was an intruder in her hotel room, it was too late to scream. In the light of the pale Hawaiian moon filtering through the window she saw a small, blunt object in the stranger's hand. A gun?

"Come in and close the door. Quietly." The man's voice floated across the room to her in tones of darkness and dominance, reaching her with the impact of an uncoiling whip.

Frozen in the doorway, Hannah stared, trying to discern his features in the shadows. Her first reaction after the initial fear was bewilderment. "I know you," she heard herself whisper shakily. "You were on the plane yesterday."

"Close the door, Miss Prescott." The man had been crouching beside one of her suitcases. He got to his feet with slow intent as she continued to stand like a startled doe in the doorway.

His right hand moved in the dim light, and Hannah's fear-induced trance broke long enough for her to decide that the odds were just as good if she ran for her life as they were if she stayed and awaited her fate. She whirled to flee.

He was upon her before she could get back out through the door. A hard palm clamped fiercely across her mouth and a sinewy arm wrapped around her waist.

"Damn it, you're soaking wet!" the man complained gruffly as the outline of her still-damp swimsuit was imprinted on his shirt. "Just my luck. The first time I get my hands on you, you're fresh out of a pool!"

Hannah struggled wildly, feeling horribly vulnerable in her brilliant purple bikini. The suit had been bought expressly for the South Pacific tour and covered a good deal less of her rounded curves than the more prosaic one-piece she had left at home.

In her frantic efforts to free herself, the small, triangular patches of fabric that covered her breasts began to shift disastrously. Hannah was unaware of the precarious position of the bikini bra. All she knew was the superior strength in the large hands of the man who was half dragging, half carrying her toward the bed. He held her with an efficient, professional grasp that left her unable to find her balance or do any real damage in return.

"Stop struggling," the intruder ordered roughly. "Don't make me hurt you."

She wanted to scream and couldn't because of the hand across her mouth. It was like a dark, perverted nightmare, Hannah realized in panic. This was the man she had fantasized about yesterday on the airplane; the one who had caught her attention even as he'd casually walked down the aisle to take a seat a few rows behind her. It had been such a harmless, gentle fantasy. A feminine day-

dream. Never in the course of that daydream had she
imagined this kind of violence. How could a fantasy go so
darkly awry?

She fought desperately, using her sandal-clad feet to kick
at him and her nails to rake his arm, but she fought inef-
ficiently and unskillfully. The stranger seemed to realize
that her frantic efforts to free herself weren't going to stop
at his command. Ruthlessly he pinned her to the bed, his
palm still sealing her mouth.

Hannah was terrifyingly aware of the heavy weight of
the hard body anchoring her to the beige bedspread. He
was using his strength to crush her into submission.

"Calm down, you little hellcat. I won't hurt you if you'll
just behave yourself. I'm here for the goddess!"

The goddess? He wasn't merely an intruder, Hannah
realized, he was an insane intruder. How did one handle a
crazy man bent on assault? Eyes wide and fearful, she
stared up at him in the moonlight, temporarily ceasing her
struggles. She must remain calm, she told herself, encourage him to at least release her mouth. Perhaps then she
could manage a scream for help. He didn't seem to be using the object she had assumed was a gun. Maybe he was
unarmed after all. She might have a chance. The possibility gave her the first ray of hope she'd had since she'd en-
tered the room.

"That's better," the man growled as she went quiet beneath him. He made no immediate effort to move, continuing to let his hard weight sprawl across her softness.
"You'd think I was trying to rape you, the way you're
struggling. Such a fierce little thing. But you're much too
soft for this kind of battle. A man only has to put his
hands on you in order to either crush you or make love to
you."

Hannah saw the way his eyes moved from her panic-
stricken gaze, down the length of her throat to the area

where her purple bikini should have been covering her breasts. It was then that she realized how the bra cups had slipped, exposing the rounded, high-crested globes. The tension in her body reached an even higher level. In the moonlight she could see the way his gaze lingered. The silent menace in the room was palpable.

Then, very slowly, the man moved one hand from her wrists to the scraps of purple fabric lying alongside her breasts. With care and a curious precision, as if he didn't quite trust himself to do the job properly, he slipped the bra back into position. Hannah's eyes closed briefly in silent relief. Surely if he had been bent on rape he wouldn't have made such a concession to modesty.

"I don't want to hurt you," the man stated quietly.

Trapped as she was beneath him, Hannah didn't believe the words, and her reaction showed in her eyes. A strange smile flickered around the edge of his mouth and then disappeared.

"I mean it, Hannah Prescott. I don't want to have to use force. And I'm not here to rape you." His hand moved with almost casual interest across her stomach and then went back to anchoring her wrists. "Although I have to admit that the idea of making love to you is rather intriguing. I wonder how you'd feel if you were clinging to me instead of struggling," he added whimsically. "Are you soft all the way through, or is it only on the surface? Have you ever needed a man, Hannah, or do you just use them?"

Crazy. Hannah continued to stare up at him with bewilderment, anger, and fear. The man was absolutely crazy. God help her; she had fallen into the hands of a madman.

"Are you going to behave?" he asked calmly.

She nodded at once. Her assailant looked skeptical, as well he might. Hannah fully intended to scream her head off as soon as he released her mouth. In the shadows she could make out the harsh lines of his face as he studied her. Eyes that were almost the color of gun-metal in moonlight watched her intently for a moment longer as if trying to read her mind, and then he slowly removed his hand.

"One false move, Miss Prescott, and I'll put a gag in your mouth and tie you to the bed with my belt. Understood?" he asked just before he freed her lips.

Hannah reconsidered her decision to scream. There was something about the cold, threatening way he spoke that convinced her he meant what he said. Perhaps it would be better to obey him for the moment. After all, he was giving her a certain amount of freedom. And one could never tell with crazies. He might calmly wring her neck after she screamed. Hannah lay on the bed, unmoving except for the fine tremor of fear that gripped her body.

"Okay, I think we understand each other." The intruder sat up warily, clearly ready to pounce if she tried anything suspicious. "Like I said, I'm not here to hurt you. I just want to know where you fit into the scheme."

"Wh—what scheme?" Her voice was a weak whisper, as if it had been a long time since it had been used.

"Look, honey, I suggest we don't waste a lot of time playing games. It's almost midnight already. I know about the goddess. What I want to know is where you fit into this. I thought the Clydemores worked alone."

"The Clydemores!" Hannah stared at him, dumbfounded. "John and Alice?"

"Who else?" The man shrugged as he continued to study her. "If it will help speed this up a bit, you can rest assured I'm not a Customs agent."

Hannah blinked in bewilderment. "I didn't think you were." She sat up very carefully, anxious not to provoke him into grabbing her again. As she moved she saw in his hand the object that she had mistaken for a weapon. It was a small wooden statue that hadn't fit into her souvenir suitcase. She had stashed it in her bag with some lingerie. The realization that this man had been going through her panties and bras made her distinctly uncomfortable.

"Ah, then you know who I am?" A flickering smile edged the man's mouth.

"You...you were on the plane with our tour group yesterday when we flew here to Hawaii from that last island."

"You handled yourself beautifully going through Customs. An incredible performance. I was very impressed. Where did you learn that delightfully scatterbrained, exhausted tourist effect? Worked like a charm. They didn't even give your bags more than a cursory glance, did they?"

In spite of her predicament, Hannah flushed in the moonlight. "That was not an act," she declared huffily, then realizing that made her sound even more scatterbrained. "I just don't happen to be a very sophisticated traveler. This ten-day South Pacific tour is my first trip out of the continental U.S."

"Beautiful," he murmured.

"Who? Me?"

"No, the act."

Hannah nodded. "I didn't think you meant me. Would you mind telling me what this is all about? Are you here to steal something?"

"You've already done the stealing. I'm here to get the stolen merchandise back for its rightful owner." The man rose from the bed and moved across the hotel room to switch on a light. "Now that we've established my reason for being in your room, I don't think you'll resort to screaming. You don't want the attention of the authorities any more than I do."

Hannah stared at him as he dropped down beside her suitcase again. "I don't?" she asked blankly. She didn't sense any immediate threat in his action. The stranger seemed totally concerned with the suitcase full of souvenirs. He was idly flicking the combination lock.

"It would be a little difficult to explain the goddess, wouldn't it? And if you force me into it, I'll tell the authorities about her. I'm willing to handle the whole thing quietly if you'll cooperate, but otherwise..." He let the sentence trail off significantly while glancing at her over his shoulder.

"I see." Hannah swallowed uncertainly, frowning at his hard, lean frame as he crouched beside the case. A thought struck her. "Are you a cat burglar?"

"No. I'm just not particularly fond of Customs agents and related types. What's the combination of the lock, Miss Prescott?"

"Why? There's nothing but souvenirs in that suitcase."

"I'm a great collector of souvenirs."

"If you'll leave my room, you can take the whole bag full of them!" she snapped, regaining some of her composure as she realized she didn't seem to be in any personal jeopardy. Yet. The man didn't really look crazy. He looked determined, but not irrational. But then why was he so concerned with a suitcase full of souvenirs collected on a ten-day whirlwind tour of the South Pacific?

Actually, if she'd been asked to guess his occupation yesterday when he'd boarded the plane, she would have said he wasn't the type to break into hotel rooms and pry into suitcases.

But then, Hannah Prescott always tended to believe the best of everyone until something happened to prove her wrong. And in this case, when she had actually found herself strangely aware of the man as he'd walked down the center aisle of the jet to take his seat, she definitely would not have wanted to believe him a criminal. She had sat in her seat and fantasized about him surreptitiously watching her just as she was watching him. Hannah was practical enough to realize that was a highly unlikely possibility, but she was enough of a dreamer to let herself spin a quick fairy tale. She rarely saw men about whom she wanted to dream.

What an idiot she had been! He probably *had* been watching her, but not because of any instantaneous chemical attraction. He had been plotting to steal her bulging bag full of souvenirs.

"Why?" she asked in growing confusion. "I mean, you're welcome to them, but why would you want them? You don't really look like the kind of man who takes home a lot of souvenirs when he travels.

"The combination, Miss Prescott?" He tapped the lock meaningfully.

"Five-four-three," she mumbled.

He nodded. "Thank you. That will save us some time." He quickly spun the dials.

"You seem to know my name," Hannah began carefully.

"If you want to know mine, it's Jarrett Blade." He didn't seem to care one way or the other, but he glanced up briefly to see if there was a flash of recognition on her face. He smiled again as she frowned. "You really are very good at the dumb tourist bit. If I didn't know better, I would have bought the act myself."

"I am not a dumb tourist!" she felt obliged to declare. "I may look a bit frazzled, but I'm at the end of a very full tour. Hawaii is the last stop before I go home to Seattle. In the past week I've been to New Zealand and so many islands I've forgotten the names of half of them. You'd look a little dumb and scatterbrained too if you'd been on the hectic schedule I've been on for the past week."

That wasn't precisely true, she realized. There wasn't much that would ever make this man look dumb or scat-

terbrained. Jarrett Blade had a cool, restrained aura of
self-control that bordered on raw power. Yesterday she had
only seen him for a few moments, time enough to notice
the compelling gray eyes and the somber brown hair with
its flecks of gunmetal gray. He had walked down the aisle
of the plane with a strong, graceful stride, and she had
dared to stare for a few seconds at the hard profile.

Blade was a good name for him, she decided now. A
man of tempered steel. A man with a cutting edge that
could slice a woman or an enemy to ribbons. How could
she have been even briefly attracted to someone as cold and
alien as this man?

As he deftly manipulated the lock of the suitcase, Hannah knew a sense of wry wonder at her initial fantasies
about Jarrett Blade. Look at him, she thought. He looks
as if he's spent his life totally alone. The kind of man who
simply doesn't need anyone else. There was no suggestion
of charm in the unhandsome, bleakly carved features, no
hint of warmth or compassion in those strange gray eyes.
Dressed in khaki slacks and a cotton shirt of the same
color, Jarrett Blade looked at home here in Waikiki. He
was the kind of man who would look assured and in control anywhere he chose to be.

While she looked frazzled and scatterbrained.

What a silly fantasy she had indulged in yesterday on the
return flight to the States. Imagine having had even the
briefest of daydreams about a man like this. Definitely not
her type.

"Be careful!" she yelped as the last digit of the combination fell into place.

Her instinctive cry of warning came too late, however.
The suitcase, which had been packed to the brim and shut
with great effort, sprang open as the catch was released.
The contents seemed to leap out of the bag as it flew open.
A bundle of cloth printed in a wild, exotic pattern, several

clay statues of various island gods, a heavy Tahitian danc-
ing skirt, a bunch of shell necklaces, and a grotesque little
purse trimmed in beads and shells fell out on the floor.
There was a great deal more of the same still inside the
suitcase.

"Quite a collection," Jarrett Blade observed, reaching
out to pick up one of the small clay statues. "You must
have spent most of the trip in the various island markets.
It looks like you've got every bit of junk manufactured on
every island in the Pacific."

"It's not junk! Those are souvenirs of a trip I'll always
want to remember. I may never get to the South Pacific
again. I almost didn't make it this time."

"No?" He sounded skeptical as he studied the small
statue in his hand.

"I lost my job just before I was scheduled to leave ten
days ago," Hannah explained sadly. "I should have cashed
in my ticket and saved the money until I found another
position, but I'd been looking forward to the trip for so
long I just couldn't bring myself to do it."

"I'll bet you couldn't." He spoke almost absently, his
attention still on the small clay god. Then, as Hannah
watched with horrified eyes, Jarrett lifted the statue high
in the air and brought it down sharply against the tile floor
of the room. The little object shattered into several pieces.

"Hey! What do you think you're doing?" she squeaked.
"That cost me three and a half dollars!" Maybe he really
was crazy!

"You didn't really intend to drag all this junk back from
Hawaii, did you? You only needed it as a cover to get
through Customs."

"No! Wait a minute!" Hannah gasped as he picked up
a small statue of a laughing creature with a huge tummy.
Jarrett ignored her, rapping the second statue sharply on
the tile. It, too, shattered.

Maybe she could edge toward the door and make her escape while he was methodically smashing her souvenirs, Hannah thought on a rising note of hysteria. Her pulse pounding as she acknowledged that she must, after all, be dealing with a maniac, she skittered a couple of inches across the bed.

"Don't get any ideas. You're not going anywhere." Jarrett didn't even bother to glance in her direction. He was reaching for the next statue.

"Mr. Blade," Hannah managed, trying for a soothing, placating tone, "I'm very sorry if you have something against little clay statues. You're welcome to smash all of them, if you like, but you really don't need me around while you do it. Take the lot of them. Wouldn't you really rather smash them in privacy?"

"You could save me some time by pointing out which one is the goddess," Jarrett told her calmly as the third statue disintegrated beneath his hands.

"The goddess? Yes, well, uh, perhaps the little doll with the tapa cloth skirt?" she suggested weakly, indicating one of the remaining souvenirs. It was a wild guess, of course. The doll, as far as Hannah knew, was not meant to represent a goddess. It was merely a toy. Dear Lord, she thought frantically, which of her souvenirs looked most like a goddess? And what in the world would this man want with such a thing? Crazy. Jarrett Blade was out of his mind.

"The little island-girl doll? Okay." He picked it up and promptly rapped the small plastic toy against the tile. It didn't shatter, but it did crack along the length of the body. Jarrett pulled it apart to reveal a hollow interior.

"There! Now she's destroyed. Your mission is accomplished," Hannah announced, trying for a bright voice. "She's quite dead. You can leave now. Go back to your room. Rest assured that the goddess will never bring bad

luck again to anyone." Was that the right sort of patter for
soothing an escaped mental patient who had a thing
against island gods and goddesses? Maybe she should take
another approach. She could try telling him that the goddess had escaped from the suitcase during the day....

"It's a matter of opinion whether she brings bad luck,"
Jarrett said coolly, pawing through the remaining souvenirs. "Some women may have thought so, of course, but
generally speaking, most people probably held her in rev-
erent awe. Ancient primitive people had a different view of
childbirth. They knew that bringing forth children wasn't
a casual matter to be taken for granted. It was an act of
powerful magic. The goddess would have been wooed with
sacrifices and much reverence, I imagine."

Feeling as if she had been caught in a degenerating
wonderland, Hannah watched Jarrett through widening
eyes. "Yes, yes, of course," she agreed faintly. "Uh, perhaps she escaped from the suitcase, Mr. Blade. After all,
a powerful goddess would have found it easy to pick that
lock and get out, don't you think?"

"Not without a bit of help, and I've been watching this
room all day. She didn't get any assistance."

"Oh." Hannah found herself stumped for a more intelligent response. He'd been watching the room all day? And
to think that yesterday she had been indulging in romantic fantasies of having him notice her! Right now she'd sell
her chance at another job back in Seattle if it meant being
free of this man.

Tonight, his gaze was deeply disturbing, especially when
it settled on the too-small purple bikini! Her cognac-brown
hair was in its usual braided coronet, making it appear that
the only thing she had on beside the skimpy bathing suit
was a crown. But Hannah felt very underdressed for any
regal occasion.

The crown of hair framed an attractive face that was kept from any dramatic beauty by a scattering of freckles and a sweetly wholesome look. Hannah had assumed that the disgustingly healthy, wholesome look might disappear as she neared thirty, and she had hoped the freckles would follow. But she was twenty-nine now, and neither attribute showed any sign of fading.

Intelligence and a faintly amused, good-natured appreciation of life were apparent in her aqua-green eyes. Hannah smiled readily, and there was blazing warmth in the expression when she did so, a warmth that filled her life with friends, if not lovers.

The basic warmth in her smile seemed to be echoed in the soft, full curves of her body. Hannah was not really plump, but there was an appealing roundness to her that held a certain attraction for some men. With one dramatic exception, however, Hannah had rarely been attracted in turn.

She had spent her adult years coming to the conclusion that whatever it was she had been looking for in a man, it was either exceedingly rare or didn't exist at all. She had long since decided she was probably being far too choosy, but somehow she couldn't bring herself to settle for less. The strange part was that she was unable to put into words exactly what it was that she sought. Hannah only knew that she had never been lucky enough to find it.

And time was slipping past. In another year she would be thirty. Even though she hadn't yet reached the symbolic age, Hannah had already consciously accepted the fact that she might never marry. And even if she did, it might be far too late to risk starting a family. The freckles on her nose contained no magic power to keep her young until the right man came along.

Men like Jarrett Blade never had freckles, Hannah found herself thinking gloomily as she watched him going through her bags. Even if they were crazy. How old was he? she wondered. She estimated his age at somewhere over thirty-five and less than forty. Had he spent his life in mental institutions, or had he only recently developed this problem with goddesses?

It seemed distinctly unfair that the one man who had called to her senses in years was demented and potentially violent. What hostile fate had put her in Jarrett Blade's path?

"We're wasting time," Jarrett pointed out, interrupting her thoughts. "It would be a whole lot easier if you just told me which one was the goddess."

"Well, I'm, uh, not exactly sure, you see," Hannah began awkwardly, frantically trying to think of a way to handle this bizarre situation. "Perhaps you'd like to take the whole suitcase full of souvenirs back to your room and go through each item at leisure? That way you could be certain you got the right goddess."

"Are you so willing to give me all this junk because the goddess isn't in here?" he asked, arcing one dark brown brow. "Is she in another case after all? I assumed she was mixed in with the rest of these trashy souvenirs, but..."

"They are not trashy!" Dammit, why did she feel compelled to defend her taste in souvenirs?

"Quit playing games, Miss Prescott. I'm not leaving without the goddess." Jarrett went back to smashing items from the suitcase.

"Please...I really don't know what you're talking about. Take anything you want, but just leave!" Hannah broke off abruptly, a startled frown crossing her features as Jarrett lifted a new item out of the suitcase. It was a clay statue, not unlike those he had smashed earlier, but she honestly didn't remember buying this one. Of course, she had picked up so many last-minute things during the past several days it was entirely possible she had forgotten this ugly little creature.

"Now this one feels about right," Jarrett murmured, staring at the clay object with an intensity that made Hannah more nervous than ever.

Things were bad enough with his looking for the mysterious "goddess," but what was he liable to do when he found it? That unnerving question flashed into Hannah's mind just as Jarrett very gently fractured the badly modeled souvenir.

"Ah!" The soft, indrawn sigh came from Jarrett as the clay shards fell away to reveal something that gleamed richly in his hands.

Hannah stared, transfixed, as her midnight visitor carefully flicked off the remaining bits of clay. "A statue within a statue?" she whispered.

"Not a particularly novel way of disguising her, but then, who would think of going through all these other damn souvenirs to get to her?" Jarrett remained where he was, crouched on the floor. He turned the small, gleaming object over and over in his hands with a reverence that made Hannah chew nervously on her lower lip.

She had thought him cold and alien until now, but in this moment Hannah realized that Jarrett Blade had another side to him, a side that breathed a soul-stirring intensity and hinted at deep passions.

And he had saved it all for the gleaming object cradled in his palms. Hannah shuddered. Just her luck that the only interesting man she'd seen on the entire trip had a souvenir fetish.

That thought brought another, more disturbing realization. How had the object of Jarrett Blade's strange desire gotten into her suitcase?

"I....I really don't know where that came from," she began earnestly.

"I do."

"Well, you're certainly welcome to it," Hannah went on quickly.

"You're very generous," he drawled, tearing his fascinated gaze away from the gleaming thing in his hand long enough to send her a derisive glance.

"What's one souvenir more or less?" she tried to say heartily. "Take it. Do whatever you want with it. Just get out of here and leave me alone."

Slowly Jarrett got to his feet, ignoring the array of broken souvenirs on the floor. Holding the gleaming object in both hands, he sank down into a chair and continued to study it intently. "She's magnificent. Absolutely magnificent."

In spite of her precarious situation, Hannah found herself following the direction of his gaze. Jarrett was holding his treasure up to the light, and she could see that it was another little statue. But it wasn't made out of clay or wood. If she hadn't known better, Hannah would have said that the object was made out of gold. Deep, burnished, ancient gold.

"Not very attractive, is she?" Hannah said with an attempt at humor as she studied the golden statue. It appeared to be a representation of a woman crouched on her haunches, giving birth. There was a round fullness to every aspect of the statue. Clearly, it had been modeled by an artist who understood femininity in fundamental terms. The power of the female body as it brought forth life was in every line of the straining form.

"She wasn't meant to be beautiful," Jarrett said simply. "She was meant to induce fertility, to create new life. That sort of power transcends mere beauty. Whoever created this understood that."

Hannah cleared her throat, at a loss as to what to do or say next. "How...how did you know she was in among my souvenirs? What are you going to do with her? Is that real gold? Where is it from? How did it get in my bag?''

Folding his hands carefully around the birth deity, Jarrett looked at Hannah as she sat stiffly on the edge of the bed. Her wet swimsuit had left a damp spot on the bedclothes, and she felt increasingly uncomfortable as the suit dried on her body.

"I was going to ask you a few of those questions," Jarrett said far too gently. "Some of them I can answer myself, of course. Yes, the gold is real, but you already know that. You must know where she came from, too. South America. Peru, to be exact. She belongs to a friend of mine, and that's who I'll be giving her back to eventually. Now, suppose you answer the other questions?''

"I don't understand," Hannah gasped. "Is she stolen? Are you from the police?''

"Yes, she's stolen, as you very well know. And I've already told you I'm not from Customs or any other policing agency. Like you, I prefer not to deal with such folk any more than is absolutely necessary. I must congratulate you, Miss Prescott. You almost made it back to Seattle with her. If it weren't for the fact that I know about the Clydemores and their rather extensive interest in South American antiques, I would never have guessed you might be involved. You really don't look the type.''

"The type for what?" Hannah demanded.

"The type to smuggle such things as this little goddess." Jarrett shrugged mildly. "It's amazing. With that sincere expression in those blue-green eyes and that charmingly bedraggled, beaten tourist air about you, I'll bet you could get the Mona Lisa through Customs undisguised. I watched your whole act yesterday as we went through the formalities. Very impressive.''

"There's no call to sit there and insult me! *You* appear to be the thief around here, not me!''

"I'm merely going to return some stolen property. But first I'd like to know exactly where you fit into the picture, Miss Prescott. I can't quite figure you out. I was so sure the Clydemores worked alone...."

"Why do you keep bringing John and Alice Clydemore into this? They're a very nice couple I met in Tahiti. They've been wonderful to me!" As she talked, Hannah began once more to edge across the foot of the bed toward the door. If she were quick enough, she might be able to get the door open and run out into the hall before he could get across the room.

"Are you going to pretend you didn't know that the Clydemores' current world tour included a stay in South America?" Blade looked lovingly down at the gold birthing goddess. It was probably the only thing he looked at lovingly, Hannah told herself. "We all know how difficult it is now to get this sort of thing across the Mexico–U.S. border these days. Much easier to reroute stolen antiquities through other countries. Who would look for pre-Columbian art in the bags of tourists returning from the South Seas? The Clydemores are professionals."

"You sound quite admiring!"

"I'm capable of appreciating a good scheme to get items like this into the U.S. art market. I understand the lure of such objects," he added softly.

Hannah stared at him. He did seem to be enthralled with the little gold goddess. She found herself wondering if Jarrett Blade had ever been that enthralled with a real live woman. Well, perhaps it would work in her favor. If he continued to study the object so intensely, he wouldn't notice her slipping to the very edge of the bed.... Hungrily she cast a quick glance at the door.

"The Clydemores were smart to latch on to someone with your charmingly naive expression," Jarrett went on thoughtfully. "In spite of their cleverness, it's better not to take unnecessary chances. Letting you carry the goddess through Customs was a wise move. Who would suspect you of being capable of smuggling?"

"You, apparently!"

"Only because I've observed how close you've been to the Clydemores since yesterday. You sat next to them on the plane, had dinner with them last night, and breakfast with them again this morning. I overheard you planning an excursion into downtown Honolulu with them today. It was obvious you were probably working with them."

"I am not working with anyone! I'm not working at all, in fact! I don't even have a job to go back to!"

"The proceeds from this little lady would keep you for quite a while. There wouldn't be any need to take a nine-to-five job, would there?"

"I wouldn't know about that! If you want my opinion, it's not a pleasant sort of statue. Not at all the kind of thing I'd want sitting on my coffee table. Who'd buy it?"

"I would. If it didn't already belong to a friend of mine who wants it back," Jarrett said simply.

"Look, take the dumb thing. I don't want it, and I honestly don't know how it got into my suitcase. I just want to be left alone, okay?"

"I'm afraid I can't do that." Blade sounded genuinely regretful. "My curiosity is aroused, you see. I really do want to figure out your role in the current smuggling market. We might run into each other again, you see."

"Not if I can help it!" At her wit's end, Hannah leaped for the door. Her single advantage, she knew, lay in the fact that Jarrett Blade seemed compelled to treat the gold goddess with reverence. He wouldn't be able to just toss it aside in order to pursue her. She would gain precious seconds while he carefully set it down.

"Oh, no, you don't!" he snapped behind her as she flung open the door and raced out into the hotel hall. But he was several steps behind.

There was someone at the far end of the hall, Hannah realized. She would scream for help, call for a security guard. She ran barefoot down the corridor for several paces, opening her mouth to shout for assistance. The words were on the tip of her tongue when the breath went out of her lungs. Jarrett Blade had thrown an arm around her midsection, yanking her still-damp body back against his hard one.

Desperately Hannah gasped for breath, determined not to let her chance of escape go down the drain. But even as her mouth opened once more, her lips were crushed beneath those of her captor.

Hannah was paralyzed by the totally unexpected assault. She had expected to be physically restrained, to have a palm clamped across her mouth, even to be knocked unconscious. She hadn't expected to be kissed into submission. Indeed, if anyone had asked her about it before the event, she would have stated unhesitatingly that it is physically impossible to be kissed into submission.

Now she knew differently.

Jarrett crowded her soft body back against the corridor wall, his mouth fastened on hers with an intensity that literally left her breathless. His hands locked into the neat coil of braids on her head, forcing her to hold still for the overwhelming embrace. With ruthless intent, his leg pushed between her bare thighs, leaving Hannah feeling ravished and helpless.

Her fingers dug into the fabric of his khaki shirt in an instinctive movement of defense. But if he felt the punishment of her nails on his shoulders, he gave no sign.

Barely able to breathe, her body completely captive in the grip of Jarrett's superior strength, Hannah endured the endless, silencing kiss. Dimly she heard the passing of other people in the hall. She knew they must have smiled to themselves and turned politely away from the scene Jarrett was creating, but she was incapable of appealing for assistance.

Hannah's body shuddered beneath the force being unleashed against her. Her head spun with the kaleidoscope of sensations that poured over her and through her. The kiss was meant to silence and punish. Jarrett demanded no other response but surrender. Out of some primitive female instinct of self-protection, Hannah gave in to him. She allowed her body to go limp and acquiescent, and she parted her teeth for the invasion of his tongue.

Jarrett seemed to crowd even closer as she gave ground before his assault. He seized the territory she yielded, conquering and claiming until Hannah felt she had given him everything she had.

It was only as she stopped fighting him that she began to sense that Jarrett Blade was not unaffected by the scorching embrace. When her body softened against his, she realized just how hard and urgent his own was. When her mouth yielded to his, she became conscious of more than mere dominance in his kiss. For a blinding moment Hannah thought she was experiencing a fragment of the deep passion she had sensed in Jarrett Blade when he had cradled the birthing goddess in his hands.

That was impossible, of course. The man was only trying to restrain her in the most effective way he could devise. But just for an instant she could have sworn she experienced something else in his arms: a frighteningly heady emotion that she could only be grateful was not totally released.

How long she stood locked against him, Hannah never knew. But when Jarrett finally lifted his mouth from hers, she was panting as if she had just run a marathon. Wide-eyed and wordless, she looked up at him. His face was an unreadable mask, although she was still fiercely aware of the tension in his body.

"If you run from me again," he grated, "I'll turn you over to Customs. I'll tell them how I found the statue in your bag, and i'll leave you to talk yourself out of the situation. Do you understand? You will do as I say, Hannah Prescott, or I'll see to it you wind up explaining everything to the authorities."

"But I haven't done anything!" she wailed, feeling trapped.

"You think they'll believe you after I've shown them the goddess?" He clamped his hands around her bare shoulders, giving her a small shake.

"You...you're threatening me!" she gasped.

"You're very perceptive!"

"But I'm innocent!" How could she have gotten herself into such a situation? She'd never come close to a brush with the law in her entire life. Her aqua-green eyes shimmered with bewildered anxiety and her bruised mouth trembled. "I didn't steal that stupid statue! I've never stolen anything in my whole twenty-nine years!"

"Are you trying to tell me the Clydemores used you? That you had no notion of what was going on?" he rasped.

"Yes!"

There was a tense pause as he stared down at her up-turned face. Hannah felt as if her whole future was suddenly hanging in the balance. This man held her in the palm of his hand, just as he'd held the statue.

"Prove it," Jarrett finally whispered.

She blinked uncomprehendingly. "Prove what?"

"That you're not involved with the Clydemores."

"But how?" Her plea was a cry of helpless frustration. How could she prove anything with that damaging bit of evidence in her suitcase?

"I'll set up a way for you to show me you're not working with the Clydemores," he told her evenly. "But it won't work unless you're telling me the truth."

"How can I prove anything?"

"Leave the how of it to me." He stepped away from her, taking her elbow firmly and guiding her back to her room.

Hannah caught her breath as a realization dawned on her. "You don't really want to turn me over to the authorities, do you? You want that statue for yourself!"

"What I want doesn't come into it at the moment," he retorted coolly. "Believe me, I won't hesitate to hand you over to Customs if you try to escape again. Are we very clear on that point?"

She slanted him a sullen, seething glance. "You've made yourself very clear, Mr. Blade."

"Good. With a woman it's always best to have everything on the table, I've found. Never allow any loopholes. Women will find loopholes in a relationship faster than the IRS will find mistakes on a tax form."

"We don't exactly have a relationship!" Hannah bit back, stung.

"But that's just exactly what we do have, Hannah," he murmured as he pushed her into her hotel room. "Beginning tonight, you and I have a relationship. And after that kiss in the hallway, I'm inclined to think it won't be platonic, either."

Two

"Don't look so shocked, Hannah." Jarrett dropped lightly back into the chair he had occupied earlier. The little gold goddess sat on the table beside him, light gleaming from its time-smoothed surface. The statue's gaze seemed to be focused on Hannah as she moved uneasily around the small room. "Our 'relationship' is the way I'm going to keep track of you while you prove you're not involved with the Clydemores. We have to have some way of accounting for my constant presence in your vicinity, don't we? We'll let John and Alice think you're having a vacation fling. How much longer are you due to stay in Hawaii?"

"Four more days," she muttered.

"That doesn't give us much time, does it? You may have to extend your visit."

"That's impossible. I have responsibilities back in Seattle. I can't stay away any longer than the time I originally planned!"

"What responsibilities? You told me you lost your job just before you left." Jarrett gave her a cold smile. "Is there a man waiting for you, Hannah?"

Angrily she looked away from him. "I have no intention of explaining my whole life to you. Just tell me how I'm supposed to prove I'm innocent of stealing your friend's statue, and let's get on with it."

Jarrett studied her for a moment as she moved restlessly about the room. "If you're not involved in the theft and if the Clydemores planted the statue in your bags so that you could take the risk of smuggling it through Customs for them, then we have to assume they'll want to retrieve the goddess before you go home to Seattle."

Hannah frowned. "Well, yes, I suppose so. The Clydemores told me they live in San Diego."

"They do. Soon you'll all be going your separate ways. That means that sometime in the next few days the Clydemores will have to find a way of getting the statue out of your luggage. It will be interesting to see what they do when they discover it's not there."

Hannah licked her lower lip. "And if they don't make an attempt to steal the statue from my luggage?"

"Then we'll have to assume that you are working with them and that they plan on letting you carry it all the way back to the mainland. If they allow you to take it home, then I'll have to believe they intend seeing you again, won't I? That you are, in fact, a partner in their little scheme."

"You're saying that the only way I can convince you I'm innocent is if the Clydemores make an attempt to get that statue back before I leave for Seattle. What if they don't make the attempt? You're just going to assume that's evidence I'm working with them?"

"Makes sense, don't you think?"

"But that leaves me at the mercy of fate. Maybe the Clydemores won't make an attempt to steal the goddess back. Maybe they weren't the ones who put it in my luggage in the first place. Maybe they're innocent too! Have you thought of that?'' she demanded wildly.

"Then you're going to look like the only guilty party, aren't you?" he drawled. "But to tell you the truth, I already have some doubts about you in the role of smuggler. There's something about you that doesn't fit the image."

"I thought you'd decided my frazzled tourist act was just that—an act!"

"It probably is," he agreed too easily. "But there's just a chance you're for real. And if you are, I'm willing to be convinced of your innocence."

"Thank you very much!" she snapped scathingly. "Are you always so distrustful of other people?"

He looked at her. "Yes. Especially women. Women are so very good at deceit, you see."

"No, I don't see! Of all the prejudiced, bigoted, chauvinistic attitudes!"

"I learned my lesson the hard way, but I learned it well, Hannah. Most modern women don't seem to need a man; they just use men for various and assorted reasons."

"Meaning men don't use women?" she snapped back.

He shrugged. "It happens."

"Gracious of you to admit it. A case of self-defense, I suppose?"

"Things weren't meant to be that way, Hannah," Jarrett said intently.

"No?"

"No." He nodded toward the little goddess. "Ancient civilizations such as the one that produced that lady understood the real nature of women. And the danger in them. Women, in turn, understood that they needed men. Men protected them, provided them with homes, fathered their children, assumed the responsibilities of economic support...and kept the magic in them under control."

"In other words, the men kept the women barefoot and pregnant!" Hannah interrupted scathingly. "How perfectly ridiculous to romanticize the kind of master-slave relationship that existed between men and women in ancient times. Typical of a man to look back on such things with nostalgia. Don't expect modern women to share your point of view!"

"I'm well aware that they don't," he assured her quietly.

Hannah gave him a startled glance. "My God," she breathed with perception. "Some woman really worked you over good, didn't she?"

"I'm grateful to her. She taught me a lesson I'll never forget."

"I'll bet you don't have a lot of female friends! I can't see many intelligent women putting up with your antiquated philosophies of how a relationship between the sexes should work."

His mouth curved wryly as he acknowledged the insight. "No, I don't have a lot of female friends. At the moment I don't even have a lover. Are you interested in applying for the position?"

"Not on your life!" Hannah stormed. "Besides, if you distrust and dislike modern women so much, I'm surprised you're even interested in having one for a lover. Or are you just in the market for someone you can use the way that woman who taught you a lesson once used you?"

Jarrett's gunmetal-gray eyes hardened briefly, and he made a visible effort to relax. "I have all the normal male instincts."

"Including a few left over from primitive times?"

"Perhaps," he acknowledged.

"It's no wonder you can't find yourself a modern-day love!" A misfit, Hannah decided morosely. What a quirk of fate. The one man who had attracted her in years, and he turned out to be some kind of throwback, alienated from his own world in a fundamental way. Maybe that was why the little golden goddess held such fascination for him. She was from his era. Hannah shivered.

"I haven't led a completely celibate life, if that's what you're assuming, Hannah. But I'm damn careful what role I allow a woman to play in my life."

"In other words, you're willing to let one into your bed so that you can satisfy your physical needs, but that's as close as she can get, right?"

"That's pretty damn close," Jarrett pointed out with amusement.

"Two people can go to bed together and still be a thousand miles apart. Or a thousand years, in your case," Hannah protested, wondering how on earth she had ever gotten into such an intimate discussion with this man.

"You sound like an authority on the subject," Jarrett mused, gray eyes glittering. "What happened? Did some man invite you into his bed and then refuse to let you manipulate him? That's very frustrating for a woman, isn't it? Women prefer to be the manipulators in a relationship. At least modern women do."

It was a stupid discussion, she decided. "I didn't want to manipulate him," Hannah sighed. "I only wanted to love him and to have him love me. I only wanted a family.... He was the one who used me, if it makes you feel any better," she concluded abruptly. With the ease of long practice, Hannah pushed the bitter memories of her twenty-fourth year to the back of her mind. She certainly had problems enough at the moment. Coming to a halt in the middle of the room, she swung around to face her unwelcome visitor and found him studying her broodingly. "I think you've done enough damage this evening, Mr.

Blade. It's about time you left. Take that dumb little statue with you and get out of my room."

Jarrett rested his chin on a propped hand for a moment longer, as if he were trying to analyze something he saw in her face. Then he appeared to abandon the attempt. He got to his feet with a slow, easy movement that spoke of a strong, coordinated body. Reaching down to pick up the goddess with both hands, he walked deliberately across the room to the closed connecting door. Casually he opened it and then paused in the doorway.

"Don't look so stunned, Hannah," he said gently. "I made sure that you were assigned this room yesterday and that I got the one next to you. The desk clerk was only too happy to accept a small tip for doing me the favor of putting me next to the frazzled lady tourist with the little crown of braids."

Hannah glared at him. "That door is supposed to be locked at all times. From both sides!" He'd been right next door to her last night. An unnerving thought.

"Not while you and I are involved with each other." Jarrett held up a key and then dropped it into his pocket. "Good night, Hannah. Don't worry about the goddess. I'll take good care of her."

"Better make sure she doesn't cast any magical female spells over you!" Hannah hissed. "After all, she is a goddess, remember? A golden lady with power. You'd better be careful."

Suddenly a wide, very male grin appeared on Jarrett's harshly carved face. It startled Hannah. For an instant he looked almost likable. "You're the one who should exercise caution, Hannah. She's a fertility goddess. Her specialty was ensuring that women got pregnant. And you've been carrying her around in your suitcase for several days."

The slipper Hannah aimed at her tormentor's head struck the door instead.

Fertility goddess! So Jarrett thought that amusing, did he? That was because he believed in the old adage about keeping women barefoot and pregnant. Hannah stormed into the bathroom and turned on the shower. She wondered just what that other woman had done to him to make him so distrusting of the female sex. Was it after the fateful lesson he had learned at her hands that Jarrett had begun pouring his passion into pre-Columbian art? Because there was passion in the man. She had seen more than one hint of it tonight.

Hannah shivered beneath the warmth of the shower and stopped herself from pursuing that line of thought. No, she was most definitely not going to allow herself to dwell on the implications of Jarrett Blade's passions. If the man chose to bury himself amid the artifacts of another age, that was his problem. She was certainly not going to allow herself to feel any compassion for a man who distrusted women the way Jarrett did. He'd made his own damn bed, apparently, a long time ago.

"Let him lie in it. Alone." Hannah grimaced at herself in the steamed mirror as she stepped out of the shower. In the meantime, what was she going to do? She was in an unbelievable mess. A smuggler? Her? Only a man as cynical as Jarrett Blade could actually believe such a thing!

What now? Should she confront the Clydemores? Warn them that somebody by the name of Blade thought they were involved in a smuggling ring? If they weren't guilty of having stashed that little goddess in her suitcase, then presumably they would be safe. Jarrett could prove nothing against them. After all, he'd found the statue in her own luggage. Frowning, Hannah dried herself quickly and went back into the bedroom.

On the other hand, what if John and Alice *were* smugglers? Jarrett seemed so sure of his facts. Of course, he was also sure that all women were out to conquer and control men, too!

The guy is a first-class nut case and he's in the adjoining room! Hannah slid a nervous glance toward the closed door between the rooms. What if she simply slipped out of the hotel and headed for the airport?

No, if she fled the scene, Jarrett would be certain she was guilty. And somehow she wanted to convince him she'd known nothing about the gold goddess. It would be satisfying to have Jarrett Blade eat his accusations and suspicions.

But her only chance of proving herself innocent lay with the Clydemores. What if they made no move to retrieve the stolen figurine? Well, Jarrett probably wouldn't turn her over to the authorities. She'd sensed he really didn't want anything to do with Customs. Apparently he was acting for a friend and preferred to keep the whole shady matter quiet.

"So what does that make you, Jarrett Blade?" Hannah whispered into the darkness as she slid into bed. "Are you a smuggler yourself? Are you a thief? A private agent dealing in pre-Columbian art? Where the hell do you fit into this whole picture?"

In the adjoining room Jarrett lay in bed listening as Hannah showered and climbed into bed. The small gold figure was on the nightstand beside him, and as he listened he absently reached out a hand and stroked it. This statue was fantastic. Early Chavín goldsmithing from ancient Peru. Probably around 250 B.C. A magnificent example of the fine artistry of the Chavín culture. God, he'd give a fortune to add it to his collection.

And Hannah Prescott seemed genuinely unconcerned with it. To her the priceless statue had simply been placed in her overstuffed souvenir bag by accident. Hannah Prescott, in fact, seemed remarkably genuine all the way around. But you could never be sure with a woman.

Still, was it really possible for someone with eyes like Hannah's to lie? Jarrett's fingers tightened briefly around the body of the goddess and his thumb moved on the gold surface in an unconsciously sensual motion. He wondered what Hannah's eyes would look like filled with desire.

"Christ," he grated softly to himself. "I must be going out of my mind to even consider the possibility that she's an innocent bystander caught up in all this."

But she had felt startlingly good against him when he'd captured her and kissed her in the hall. Gentle and soft and warm. He couldn't recall being so aware of the gentleness and softness of a woman before. Certainly not during a kiss meant to threaten and control.

She was dangerous, a creature of magic and power because she gave out signals of sweet, womanly softness when he knew her to be a hard, accomplished smuggler.

At least, Jarrett corrected himself with a frown, all the evidence indicated she was a smuggler. But there was just a chance she wasn't guilty. He'd been watching her since yesterday, and for some reason he couldn't quite bring himself to believe she was a hardened thief. Dammit, he wanted her to prove herself innocent. He wanted her to be merely an unsuspecting pawn of the Clydemores. He wanted the honesty in those aqua eyes to prove genuine and he wanted the softness in Hannah Prescott to include more than just her body.

If she was an innocent victim she was going to need him to protect her from the Clydemores. And the notion of Hannah needing him was very satisfying, Jarrett decided.

Very early the next morning Hannah sat in the hotel coffee shop, gloomily stirring her coffee and trying to convince herself that the strange man who had paid her such a frightening visit in the middle of the night was only a bad dream. Unfortunately there were all those bits of broken souvenirs still lying on her floor this morning to argue otherwise.

There was no denying the fact that the small golden statue had been in her bag, and Hannah honestly could not remember having purchased the souvenir statue that had concealed it. Could Jarrett Blade possibily be right about the Clydemores? They had spent a great deal of time with her since Tahiti and they were world travelers. They knew their way around airports, Customs, and foreign hotels. Could they possibly be genuine smugglers? Had she been used by them to take the risks of getting that golden goddess through U.S. Customs?

"Good morning, Hannah."

With a wary expression Hannah lifted her eyes to find Jarrett standing at her table, about to seat himself. Jarrett Blade embodied a good lesson on the subject of wishful thinking: he proved out the old admonition about being careful what one wished for because one might get it. She appeared to be stuck with him.

"I don't suppose there's any point in my saying you're not particularly welcome to sit down and join me?" she said.

"None at all. I heard you leave the room a few minutes ago. You should have waited for me." Jarrett slid easily into the seat across from her. In the bright morning light that illuminated the terrace café he looked every bit as hard and dangerous as he had at midnight. His somber brown hair was ruthlessly combed into place and the cotton slacks and shirt he wore looked as if they had just come back from the cleaners.

"You like to control everything in your life, don't you, Mr. Blade?" Hannah was as surprised as he was to hear the comment come from her lips.

"What makes you say that?" he asked casually as a waitress poured coffee.

Hannah lifted one shoulder uncomfortably, wishing she'd kept her mouth shut. The shoulder was bare, as were her legs. The flower-spattered island dress she was wearing left a lot of her bare this morning. "Your hair's too short, as if you're afraid it might get out of line if you let it grow longer. Your clothes look as if they were just pressed, even though you're in Hawaii where that sort of thing isn't important. Even your shoes are shined. You look as if you're here on business."

"I am." He sipped his coffee and eyed her watchfully. "You're my business."

"Look, Mr. Blade, I've done a lot of thinking since last night," Hannah said earnestly, "and I have the impression you really don't want to mess with the authorities any more than I do. You've got your precious statue. Why not take it and leave me alone?"

"Because I want to know where you fit into all this."

"But why?" she demanded helplessly.

"I don't like unknown quantities. I've been aware of the Clydemores' activities for years. But you're new on the art smuggling scene. I want to know who you are and where you fit in. You're too much of a mystery lady to be left alone. I want answers."

Hannah narrowed her eyes. "I assure you the answers are going to be exceedingly dull."

"Maybe. Maybe not." He glanced up, and a satisfied expression tightened the small lines around his gray eyes. "Here come the Clydemores. Maybe we'll start getting a few of those answers now."

Hannah glanced up nervously. What should she do? Warn John and Alice that there was a crazy man in their midst? On the other hand, if the middle-aged couple were innocent they didn't need the warning, did they? Where would that leave her, though? Shouldering the entire blame for the theft of that damn fertility goddess?

As if he sensed her uncertainty and anxiety, Jarrett slanted her a chilling glance. "Just follow my lead, Hannah. That's an order."

"I didn't sign anything that says I have to take orders from you," she shot back under her breath, and she at least had the satisfaction of having had the last word. In the next instant John and Alice Clydemore descended on the table.

"Good morning, Hannah!" Alice gushed happily, her cheerful blue eyes going rapidly from Hannah's face to Jarrett's. Alice Clydemore was a handsome woman in her early sixties with a still-trim figure and stylishly silvered hair. She wore expensive resort-style clothing from a leading designer and there were several gold chains at her throat and on her wrist. "And who's this?" she asked pertly, smiling at Jarrett as she sat down.

"Richard Adams," Jarrett announced smoothly, rising to his feet politely.

Hannah nearly choked on her coffee as she heard him blithely lie about his name. She glanced up with startled eyes as the man she knew as Jarrett Blade shook John Clydemore's hand.

"Adams, hmmm?" John clarified genially, taking the seat opposite his wife. His middle-aged, patrician features matched those of his wife, handsome and politely bespeaking wealth, "Don't recall having met you. Not part of Hannah's tour group, are you?"

"No. I just happened to be on the same plane yesterday." Jarrett smiled affectionately at Hannah, who stared back at him in consternation. "I followed her through Customs and then lost her. But last night I located her at this hotel. It wasn't hard. All I had to do was ask around until I found someone who knew where her tour group had been booked."

"I smell a romance," Alice Clydemore decided in satisfaction. "How exciting! Poor Hannah's had a very dull trip so far."

"Things are livening up quite a bit," Hannah muttered into her coffee. She wished Jarrett Blade, or whatever his name was, hadn't chosen to pretend he was romantically interested in her.

"Never too late for a vacation romance," John Clydemore chuckled. "You've still got—what?—four more days in Hawaii before you go back to the mainland."

"I'll have to work fast," Jarrett drawled.

"You're also going to have to work around a few obstacles," John Clydemore said with a grin, glancing across the room to where a small family of three sat eating breakfast.

Jarrett's gaze hardened. "Other men?" Hannah didn't care for the ominous note in his voice, even if it was a faked attempt at jealousy.

Before she could answer, John was grinning even more broadly. "You could say that. One in particular, I'm afraid. Hannah has already spent several evenings with him, and he's not likely to give her up easily."

"I'll reason with him," Jarrett said coolly. "I'm sure he'll see things my way."

"From what I've seen of this young man, he's fairly stubborn. However, he's smaller than you, so..."

"So there should be no problem." Jarrett nodded as if the matter was settled.

His ridiculously possessive attitude was too much for Hannah to bear. She got to her feet. Let the Clydemores and Jarrett play silly games. She had other things to do in Hawaii.

"If you'll excuse me, I'm going down to the beach," she announced bravely, not glancing at Jarrett for his approval.

"Of course," Alice Clydemore said quickly. Then she hesitated, "Oh, by the way, Hannah, dear, I wonder if I might stop by your room this afternoon."

Hannah tilted her head uncomprehendingly. "Well, of course. Was there something you wanted to speak to me about?"

"I just wanted to take a quick look through your suitcase full of souvenirs, if you don't mind," Alice said easily. "I seem to have misplaced one of the items I picked up in Tahiti. Do you remember the night we compared purchases?"

Hannah's mouth went dry. She didn't dare look at Jarrett now. "Yes, Alice, I remember." Her fingers whitened on the back of her chair as she waited for Alice to finish incriminating herself.

"Well, I think we may have gotten a few things mixed up. I seem to have a lovely piece of tapa cloth in my suitcase that I don't remember buying and I also realized I'm missing a little clay statue I planned to take back to my granddaughter. Nothing valuable, really, but a rather cute little doll. I'm sure you wouldn't have much use for her. Do you suppose it might have gotten into your bag by mistake that evening? As I recall, we had souvenirs lying all over the hotel room that night, and it's just possible."

"It's just possible." Hannah felt unaccountably shaky. She had to get out of the restaurant. "I'll, uh, see you later, then...." Without glancing back, she hurried toward the door. En route she remembered to wave to the Tylers, the small family seated near the window, and then she was free.

Desperately she tried to think as she collected her beach
bag and a towel from her room. The little doll Alice
Clydemore seemed to think she had "misplaced" matched
the description of the one that had concealed the golden
statue. Could Jarrett be right? Were the Clydemores
smugglers?

No, they might be victims too, just like herself. Perhaps
there was someone else manipulating all three of them. She
had been traveling with the Clydemores for several days
now and felt she knew them. The one person in the whole
situation whom she barely knew at all was Jarrett Blade.
Or Richard Adams, or whoever he was. Was he the one
doing the manipulating? He said he'd just gotten on the
plane at the last stop, but who knew how long he'd been
trailing the tour.

It was all so damn confusing, Hannah decided as she
stretched out on the beach twenty minutes later. And if she
guessed right, she wasn't going to have long to consider the
problem. Jarrett Blade would probably be wandering
along any minute now. She had the impression he wasn't
going to leave her alone for long. Even as the thought
crossed her mind his voice cut through her short-lived
privacy.

"When did you get that swimsuit? When you were
twelve years old?"

"It's brand-new!" Hannah said in angry defense of the
purple bikini. She refused even to glance at Jarrett as he
casually spread a towel out beside her on the sand. But out
of the corner of her eye she could see he'd changed into a
snug-fitting pair of swim trunks that revealed the flatness
of his stomach and the muscled shape of his thighs. Hannah was appalled to find that her mind insisted on embel-
lishing the original fantasy it had begun the day before
yesterday on the plane.

"It looks as though it was designed for a scrawny twelve-year-old. You're not the scrawny type, Hannah." He stretched out beside her, critically surveying the shape of her rounded hips and breasts in the purple bikini. "I think you ought to get another suit." The final pronouncement was flat and autocratic.

Hannah's eyes flared. Enough was enough! "I really don't give a damn what sort of suit you think I ought to wear. You may be living in the past, but I'm not. This happens to be my vacation you're ruining, you know. I'd appreciate it if you'd keep your opinions to yourself. I find your threats and accusations bad enough as it is."

Jarrett considered her, leaning on one elbow as he studied her defiant expression. "You do realize that suit makes you look as though you're trolling for men?"

"So what? Maybe I am! After all, this is a vacation."

"It ceased to be a vacation the minute you got involved with the Clydemores. And you don't need to cast out any lures for strange males. You've got me now."

"A *really* strange male," she agreed in heartfelt tones.

He ignored that. "Who's this guy on the tour you've been seeing in the evenings?"

"You'll meet him tonight if you stick around," Hannah retorted with a certain relish.

"You're spending the evening with me. I'm not letting you out of my sight. Especially not after Alice Clydemore gets around to finding out that her little souvenir is no longer in your bag."

"I'm spending the evening with Danny Tyler," Hannah returned firmly. "If you insist on joining us, I suppose there's not much I can do about it. You'll probably be quite bored, however."

"Break the date."

"I can't."

"The hell you can't! You've gotten yourself mixed up in a smuggling ring, lady. If you want to prove yourself innocent, you'd better do as I say. Besides, this Tyler guy can't be very interesting if the Clydemores claim the trip has been dull for you."

"That's my business," Hannah gritted.

Without any warning, Jarrett stretched out a hand and flattened it against the gentle swell of her stomach. His eyes gleamed in the sunlight, revealing an iron will he was bent on enforcing. Hannah sucked in her breath at the touch of his fingers, every nerve in her body suddenly, throbbingly aware of him in a way she didn't wish to recognize. Mutely her eyes met his.

"Break the date, Hannah."

"What is it with you?" she whispered starkly. "Do you always have to be in charge? Do you always have to give orders? Couldn't you try making *requests*?"

His hand pressed a little harder on her bare skin, letting her know the physical strength behind the touch but not actually hurting her. He was using raw intimidation, Hannah realized angrily. And it was highly effective. She shivered.

"I told you last night that I don't want you to be in any doubt about who's in charge. Until I know for certain you're not involved with the Clydemores, I'm not taking any chances. I'm giving orders, not making requests. And you're going to obey, Hannah, aren't you?"

"If you're ever finally convinced of my innocence, am I going to get an apology? Will you give me the satisfaction of groveling at my feet?" she taunted, calling on every ounce of courage she had. It took courage to defy this man.

To her surprise, he actually considered the question. "No," Jarrett said at last. "No apology. If you aren't involved, then you should be thanking me. I'm keeping an eye on you for your own good. Who knows what the Clydemores might decide to do when they realize that statue is no longer in your souvenir bag?''

Hannah stirred beneath his touch, her uneasiness generated more by the feel of his casually intimidating hand than by any thought of what the Clydemores might do. "All right," she scoffed, "I won't hold my breath waiting for the apology. In the meantime, however, would you mind removing your hand? I'd rather you didn't touch me."

His eyes narrowed. "I like touching you. And if you're going to insist on wearing minuscule swimsuits like that one, you have to expect a certain amount of touching. Doesn't your friend Tyler put his hands on you?"

"Not frequently," she said dryly.

"Because you won't allow him to get close? Are you in control of that relationship, Hannah?"

"I make an effort to be in control, yes!" she snapped.

"Maybe you can manage the Danny Tylers of this world, but I'm different." Jarrett leaned closer, a lazily intrigued expression on his face.

Hannah caught her breath. She could smell the clean, musky scent of his body as the sun began to warm it, and she didn't like the way it sent her other senses skittering. He was going to kiss her, and Hannah was suddenly very nervous. "Jarrett, no, I don't..."

"Yes, you do. I can see it in your eyes. You have very expressive eyes, Hannah Prescott." His mouth hovered a tantalizing inch above her own. "I'm becoming more convinced by the hour that you're not a very accomplished liar."

"You, on the other hand, seem very adept at the business. You rattled off the name of Richard Adams without blinking an eye!" she accused, her body stiff and tense in the shadow of his.

"I was afraid they might recognize my real name," he said casually.

"Why? Are you also in the smuggling game?"

"Hush, Hannah." He brushed her mouth lightly.

"I don't want you kissing me or touching me or...or anything else!"

"You really are a very poor liar, honey." His mouth closed over hers.

"Hannah! Hannah, I've been looking all over for you!"

Jarrett's head came up swiftly as he glared at the six-year-old, towheaded boy who was skipping eagerly across the sand. Hannah turned her head, grateful for the interruption.

"Hello, Danny," she said quickly. "How are you this morning?"

The child came to a halt, eyeing Jarrett curiously. "I'm fine," he said politely. "Who's this?"

Jarrett looked at the boy for a moment. "My name is Jarrett. And yours is Danny?"

"Danny Tyler. Hannah's my friend," the boy added with a touch of aggression.

"So I hear. She's been telling me about you." Jarrett's voice, sounding unexpectedly reassuring, surprised Hannah. "She likes you."

Danny appeared to relax slightly. Then he sent an uncertain glance at Hannah. "Is he your friend, too?"

"Not nearly as good a friend as you are, Danny," Hannah declared roundly.

"Good enough to spend the evening with her, just as I hear you're going to do," Jarrett corrected mildly. "Are those your parents?" He glanced briefly at the young couple waving from several yards away.

"That's Mom and Dad. They're going out to dinner tonight. That's why I'm staying with Hannah. You're going to be there too, huh?"

"Do you mind?"

Danny paused while he came to a decision and then shook his head. "No, it's okay. See you later, Hannah." Danny took off in the direction of his parents, turning to wave frantically a couple of times.

Hannah sat up as Jarrett slowly pulled away. There was a thoughtful, faintly derisive expression in his eyes.

"So the mystery of Danny Tyler is solved. How long did you plan to keep stringing me along about his true role in your life?"

"As long as I could get away with it. Anything to annoy you," she added sweetly, staring fixedly out to sea.

"That's a dangerous game, Hannah."

"Annoying you? Maybe, but it's the only one in town at the moment."

"Much safer to play the game of placating me, honey." But he was smiling, she realized as she caught the curve of his mouth out of the corner of her eye. Jarrett was actually smiling. He had a weird sense of humor, she decided. "How did you get stuck baby-sitting for a six-year-old on your vacation?" he went on conversationally.

"Danny's parents had originally planned to leave their son with his grandmother, but at the last minute she got sick and couldn't take him. They had to bring him along. They were all on the same tour schedule as I was, so I got to know them. It seems that his parents had planned this trip as a second honeymoon. Having little Danny along has put something of a damper on that."

"So you let them impose on you? You've been baby-sitting for them?" he mocked.

"My evenings have hardly been full of activities on this trip. Everyone else on the tour is either married or over sixty. I haven't minded staying with Danny a few evenings so that his parents could salvage something from the trip," she shot back defensively.

"That's ridiculous," Jarrett said evenly. "You let his parents use you. Didn't you pay every bit as much for the tour as they did?"

"Well, yes, but..."

"But nothing. They had no right to corral you into baby-sitting for them. You've been used."

"You know nothing about the matter!" Hannah hissed furiously.

"It's obvious." He shrugged dismissingly. "And it's beginning to look as if the Clydemores used you, too. Does this happen a lot to you, Hannah?"

"Does what happen?"

"Do you let people use you frequently?"

"I thought you'd already decided I was a scheming, conniving user of other people," she muttered, not meeting his eyes.

"I'm beginning to wonder about you, Hannah Prescott. I'm beginning to wonder."

"Gee, thanks for that tiny vote of confidence," Hannah returned waspishly, "but it really doesn't mean much when you consider it's coming from the one person in my life who's really trying to use me—you!"

To her surprise, Jarrett's gray gaze widened in startled protest. "I am not trying to use you."

"Sure you are," she scoffed. "You're using me to prove your theories about who stole that dumb statue."

"I'm just keeping tabs on you until I know for certain what the story is," he muttered, sounding almost defensive.

"You're trying to intimidate and control me. That's another way of saying you're trying to use me. Your arrogance has to be seen to be believed, Jarrett Blade. Now would you mind shutting up for a while? I'm going to read."

It proved something of a surprise to her when he did exactly as she requested. Perhaps, Hannah decided, the trick to dealing with a man like Jarrett Blade was to take a very firm hand.

Three

——

She didn't understand, Jarrett decided as he lay watching Hannah smear suntan lotion on her rounded calves and thighs. He was only making certain that he stayed in control of a potentially dangerous situation. If she was an innocent victim of the Clydemores' manipulation, then his actions would also serve to protect her.

Women, in his experience, were generally not innocent victims, however. Elaine had been so beautiful and had claimed to love him so much that he had been unable to see the ruthless ambition in her until it was far too late. What a fool he'd been about her. But never again. Now he made certain he was always in control of himself. He never let a woman get to him in any way except the physical.

Hannah Prescott was very different from Elaine as far as looks went, Jarrett mused, his eyes continuing to follow Hannah's fingers as she stroked the lotion on her legs. Elaine had the clean, sleek lines of a thoroughbred, all long legs and elegant throat and slender body. But Hannah was soft-looking, round and full in places he found himself wanting to touch. Like the top of her legs, for instance....

"Do you want some help putting on that lotion?" he heard himself ask.

Hannah sent him a scathing glance. "No, thanks." She continued applying the suntan cream, her fingers slipping up to her bare stomach. Her skin gleamed under the fragrant oil.

Jarrett gazed at the delicate curve of her stomach and remembered how it had felt under his hand a few moments earlier. Then he followed her fingers as they moved up to anoint the upper slope of her breasts. Round and round her hands moved in smooth, sweeping patterns that left the skin glistening in their wake. Shoulders, breasts, the upper part of her arms, all seemed soft and curved and infinitely feminine. Like the utterly feminine shape of the little fertility goddess he had carefully locked away in his room, Jarrett realized.

With that realization came another. His body was hardening with alarming urgency, and the snug bathing trunks he was wearing weren't providing much concealment.

"Damn!" The short, impatient oath came from between clenched teeth as he abruptly rolled over onto his stomach.

"What's the matter?" Hannah stopped stroking her skin long enough to glance at him with a small frown.

"Nothing. Hannah, I'm serious about that bikini. I want you to wear some other suit from now on." He didn't look at her, cradling his chin on his crossed forearms. Grimly he focused on Danny Tyler, who was building a ditch together with some other children.

"Go to hell, Jarrett Blade," Hannah said lightly.

He couldn't stop himself. He knew he ought to ignore the provocation, but something in him refused to obey common sense. With a deceptive laziness Jarrett moved, shifting onto his side and angling his body very close to Hannah's. She was so startled she dropped the bottle of suntan oil. Jarrett could feel the slickness of her skin as he deliberately let his thigh come into contact with hers. Hannah's eyes opened very wide and she went quite still as she felt the heaviness of his aroused manhood through the fabric of his suit.

"Now do you understand?" he rasped, a little surprised at just how husky his voice was.

Hannah rallied quickly. "I can't help it if you have no self-control."

"You'll wear another swimsuit in the future?"

"If it will keep you from assaulting me, yes."

With a coolness he was far from feeling, Jarrett willed himself to relax. Slowly he pulled away. It took more willpower than he had anticipated to return to his own towel. But he thought he managed the feat with commendable masculine casualness. It had to look casual. The last thing he wanted Hannah to think was that he couldn't control himself at all.

"Have you ever been pregnant, Hannah?" he asked abruptly, thinking of the goddess.

She turned a faint shade of pink at the very personal question. "It's none of your business, but no, I've never had a child."

"You'd look good pregnant," Jarrett told her almost absently.

Hannah felt the embarrassed flush spreading. "Don't get any ideas where I'm concerned. I don't plan to leave Hawaii carrying your kid."

Jarrett rolled over onto his side, gray eyes meeting hers with lazy aggression. "What would you do if you went home pregnant with my baby, Hannah Prescott?"

She sucked in her breath, her whole body tensing at the cool challenge in him. Don't panic, she told herself silently. Above all, you must not panic. Don't let him rattle you. That's exactly what he's trying to accomplish. Keep your head and don't let him get away with it.

"Cry a lot," she finally suggested sarcastically. "And then file a paternity suit."

To her chagrin, Jarrett's face relaxed into a wide grin. "Make me pay through the nose, hmmm? But you wouldn't have to go to court to get me to acknowledge my responsibilities, Hannah," he added softly.

"I'll bet I would," she contradicted fiercely. "Given your distrust of women, I don't expect you'd believe any female who claimed she was pregnant by you! My God! Why am I having such a stupid conversation? Excuse me, Jarrett, I've had enough sun for today. I'm going back to the hotel!"

Leaping to her feet, she whisked her towel into her beach bag, picked up the paperback she had planned to read, and started back along the beach with a brisk, determined stride. Dammit, why had she let him goad her into such an inane discussion! Jarrett Blade had fertility goddesses on the brain.

"Hannah!"

She didn't look around as he moved smoothly to join her, but she sensed his anger.

"Hannah, don't walk away from me like that."

"Is that the only way you know how to talk, Jarrett? One order after another? One intimidating comment after another? I'll bet your social life is very limited. You make a lousy date, do you know that?"

"Unless you want to face Alice Clydemore alone when she discovers that her 'souvenir' is missing, you'd better not ditch me, lousy date though I may be," he grated, taking her arm in a grip of steel.

Hannah started to protest and then bit her lip in vexation. He was right. The last thing she wanted this afternoon was to handle Alice Clydemore alone. "Just stop talking to me as if I were some kind of female slave you have to keep in line!"

A ghost of a smile crossed his face. "I might make a lousy date, Hannah, but I have a feeling you'd make a very nice little slave girl."

She didn't smile. There was nothing at all humorous in his small joke. Resolutely she continued through the sand to the hotel entrance.

Alice Clydemore's knock came on Hannah's door just as she stepped from the shower twenty minutes later. Hastily she toweled dry and reached for a muu-muu.

"I'm coming."

The door between Hannah's room and Jarrett's opened, and she glanced up to see him standing there, his expression grim. His gray eyes glittered with anticipation. "Let her in and act as if absolutely nothing is wrong."

Hannah cast him a fulminating glance as she hurried to the door to greet Alice Clydemore. Everything was wrong, couldn't he see that? And it was all his fault!

"Hi, Alice. I just got in off the beach."

Alice smiled charmingly, nodding at Jarrett as she handed Hannah a small bundle of fabric. "I'm sorry to bother you, dear, but I decided I'd better return your tapa cloth and take a look for the little doll while I remembered it. I'd hate to get home and have to confront my granddaughter with no present! Five-year-olds aren't very understanding about such matters, you know. Hello, Richard. Did you meet your competition yet?"

"Danny and I had a little chat on the beach. We agreed to share Hannah this evening. I'm banking on the fact that I can outlast him. With any luck he'll be asleep by nine o'clock." Jarrett moved idly into the room. He was still barefoot, wearing only a pair of neatly creased slacks. He could have put on a shirt at least, Hannah thought irritably. Half naked like this, he looked far too at home in her room. What would Alice think?

"Here's the souvenir bag, Alice," she said hastily, dragging out the heavily loaded suitcase and opening it. "Take a look. I've got so much stuff in here that I'm not sure I know what's mine and what isn't. After a while all these souvenirs start to look alike, don't they?"

"You're so right, but I rather think I can remember this particular clay doll," Alice said, coming forward to begin searching through the chaos of mementos. "A fat little thing with a Tahitian skirt, as I recall..." Her hands moved more and more quickly through the jumble of items in the suitcase. A small frown began to etch her face as she failed to locate the doll. "I could have sworn I must have gotten it mixed up with your things that night we compared purchases, Hannah. Is this the lot? Any souvenirs in your other case?" She flicked a glance at the remaining suitcase.

Obligingly Hannah stepped forward to open the bag, but her palms were damp as she did so. Was Alice Clydemore really looking for that statue? Or just a missing souvenir? What was the truth of the situation? Perhaps Alice had also been duped. How did Jarrett know so much about the Clydemores? Awkwardly, her fingers trembling with nervousness, Hannah succeeded in undoing the catch.

"I don't see anything else, Alice. Want to take a look?"

Alice moved up beside her, frowning down into the case. "Well, I don't see it," she said slowly. "It must have gotten lost somewhere along the line. Are you sure this is everything? What about your beach bag?''

The beach bag, too, was opened, revealing no clay doll. Jarrett sat watching the whole process, coolly sipping from a glass of ice water he'd poured for himself. His gray gaze hovered on Alice Clydemore with something akin to satisfaction.

"It looks as though you'd better pick up something else for your granddaughter, Mrs. Clydemore," he finally drawled. "Pity to disappoint a kid."

"Yes, it certainly would be." Alice's frown cleared miraculously as she smiled at Jarrett. "I shall have to run down to one of the local souvenir shops and find something else, as you say. Well, thank you, Hannah. Sorry to bother you. You're quite sure that's everything?"

"V-very sure, Alice." Hannah didn't look at the older woman as she relatched the suitcase. "I'm sorry we couldn't find it," she offered lamely.

"No problem," Alice declared airily, heading for the door. "I'm sure I'll be able to find something else that will do. See you later. Uh, you're having dinner with Richard here, did you say?"

"And Danny," Hannah added, not quite meeting Alice's eyes. This is so awkward! she told herself.

"As I said, Danny and I will be sharing Hannah this evening," Jarrett murmured.

"I see. Well, have a lovely time. John and I are going to one of the restaurants on the other side of the island. We'll see you in the morning, then, right?"

"Right. Good-bye, Alice." Hannah shut the door behind the older woman with a shaky sense of relief and leaned back against it to stare at Jarrett. For a long moment she could think of nothing to say. Then she burst out, "Don't look so pleased with yourself! I think she's just as innocent as I am!"

"An interesting theory." He smiled. "Just another duped victim, hmm?"

"Yes, dammit!"

"You're forgetting I know something about John and Alice Clydemore."

"Such as?"

"Such as the fact that they've been involved in shady art deals for the past ten years. They've bought stuff from poor African museums, bribed border guards and museum officials, and brought it back to sell for a fortune on the U.S. art market. They've paid a few bucks to Peruvian farmers to rob ancient graves of priceless artifacts and then they smuggled the stuff out of the country and sold it for thousands. John Clydemore even got caught three years ago trying to bring illegal pre-Columbian art in through Customs in Washington D.C."

"What happened?" Hannah demanded, startled.

"Not much. He got slapped with a fine for failing to make a proper Customs declaration, and the artifacts got shipped back to the Peruvian government. Many of the emerging nations are being systematically stripped of their heritage by this kind of smuggling. They've all enacted strict laws forbidding artifacts to be exported from the country, but laws like that tend to get ignored and they're hard to enforce. Collectors are careful not to inquire too closely into the background of a particular piece of art being offered for sale. Not if they want it badly."

"You seem to know a lot about it," she charged tightly.

"I do. I have an excellent pre-Columbian collection." Jarrett bared his teeth in a brief, humorless smile.

"Then you're no better than the Clydemores," she accused.

He lifted a hand in denial. "Wrong. I'm reformed. I'll admit there was a time when I didn't inquire any more closely into the background of certain pieces than any other collector who was determined to get his hands on a certain object. And I knew where to go and who to see to get what I wanted. But I never slipped into outright smuggling. Frankly, there were easier ways of obtaining what I wanted. But now I don't even use those methods. I'm cleaner than newly fallen snow these days. I only buy pieces offered for sale by reputable dealers who have acquired them from long-standing collections."

"Don't sound so damn virtuous. I'll bet you're planning to keep that little gold fertility goddess all for yourself, aren't you?" It was a shot in the dark, but Hannah thought she detected a flicker of guilt in Jarrett's hard eyes. It was gone an instant later.

"I'm going to return that goddess to a friend of mine. I told you that. It was stolen from his collection in Peru."

"Uh-huh." She didn't bother to hide the skepticism she was feeling.

"Dammit, don't you dare accuse me of shady dealing. You're the one who's still not in the clear," he growled, surging to his feet with a restless movement. "Put your shoes on. We're going browsing or something. I don't want to sit around this hotel room all afternoon." He stalked back to his own room.

Shopping with Jarrett Blade in the countless gift and souvenir shops of Waikiki proved to be a trying experience. Hannah soon learned that the only way to keep her temper was to ignore him completely when she spotted something she wanted to buy. Jarrett simply did not share her taste in souvenirs, and he let her know it.

"Why on earth do you want that ridiculous statue of King Kamehameha?" he demanded, frowning as she selected one from the ranks of a hundred similar such carvings.

"It's made out of genuine lava!" Hannah protested, clutching the king.

"That's like saying it's made out of genuine rock. There's nothing rare or priceless about lava in Hawaii. And there's nothing rare or priceless about that statue. It was churned out on an assembly line."

"I like it and I'm going to buy it," she declared stoutly.

"It's a waste of money," Jarrett grumbled.

"Maybe, but it's legal to take back with me, unlike some of the stuff you've collected in the past!" Feeling as though she'd definitely had the last word, Hannah marched to the cashier to purchase the statue.

Matters did not improve, however. Half an hour later when she hovered over several jars of macadamia nuts, Jarrett again interfered.

"You can buy macadamia nuts back on the mainland. Why weigh down your suitcase with them?"

"Because when I get them home and eat them I'll remember that I actually bought them here in Hawaii. The same with those Maui potato chips. I'm going to take back as many bags as I can pack," Hannah informed him aggressively. "It's really none of your business, is it?"

"You're being idiotic." Jarrett surveyed the three artificial flower leis, the two hula dolls which actually did the hula when wiggled, the Kamehameha statue, and the bottle of Hawaiian flowered perfume she was already carrying. "If you want a worthwhile souvenir of the trip, let's go take a look in some of the local art galleries."

"I can't afford that sort of thing," Hannah informed him regally as she selected a bottle of the nuts.

"Well, I can, and I'm tired of browsing through all this junk. Buy the damn nuts and let's go find some good galleries."

"You go. I'd rather browse through junk."

"I'm not leaving you alone," he told her flatly.

"Then you're stuck with me and my taste in junk, aren't you?" she said, smiling kindly. "At least," she added coolly, "until you learn how to say please."

There was a distinct pause. Then Jarrett said very quietly, "Please, Hannah?"

She blinked, looking as astonished as she felt. She honestly hadn't expected him to do that. "I didn't think you'd lower your masculine ego long enough to try being civil."

Something moved in his eyes. She couldn't decide if it was annoyance or amusement. But he said nothing.

"Oh, all right," she managed rather ungraciously. "Just let me buy these nuts and I'll go with you to the art gallery."

For the next two hours she tramped around with him as he wandered through several galleries specializing in watercolors, pottery, and, to her surprise, quilts.

"Quilting? In Hawaii?" she asked, pausing before a beautifully designed coverlet.

"Umm. The missionaries taught the island women how to quilt. The women came up with their own patterns and designs. Beautiful work." Jarrett spoke almost absently as he examined the specimen in front of them.

"Hey, that's even nicer than my Kamahameha statue," Hannah decided, reaching for the price tag. "Six hundred dollars! Good grief! I could buy four hundred Kamahameha statues and a bunch of macadamia nuts for that price!" Hastily she dropped the tag and went on to the next item on display. Jarrett lingered for a while, studying the quilt.

"Look at this, Jarrett," Hannah called eagerly as she fingered some small napkin rings carved out of teak.

He glanced across the room and smiled almost indulgently. "You can buy those anywhere, honey. Besides, when was the last time you actually used napkin rings?"

"Spoilsport." She sighed and let the rings cascade back into the glass bowl that displayed them. "It's tough shopping with an art collector."

"No appreciation for the finer forms of junk, hmmm?" Jarrett laced his fingers through hers and led her through the rest of the gallery.

"Exactly." The intimate contact of his hand disturbed her. She ought to shake it off. After all, they were hardly lovers or even friends! "Souvenir hunting is an art form in and of itself, you know. You have no proper understanding of it. You've been dealing in the world of exotic art too long."

"Perhaps," he agreed, to her surprise. He paused at the cashier's desk and nodded at the woman seated behind it. "I'll take that quilt. Item number two sixty-five. Please have it wrapped and boxed for shipping by air."

"Of course, sir." The young woman beamed at him and got to her feet.

"What are you going to do with that quilt?" Hannah whispered loudly.

He slanted an unreadable glance down at her. "Make love on it," he said outrageously.

Instantly Hannah freed her hand and stepped away from him. "Well, I hope you can find a woman to share it with you," she retorted smartly. "You'll have to stop giving orders and trying to control people, though, if you expect to lure a female onto that quilt with you. Unless you're not particularly interested in a female with any intelligence, that is."

"We'll see," he said, drawing out his slim, calfskin wallet and flipping through it for a charge card.

Hannah refused to spend any more time in art galleries with him after that. Ruthlessly she insisted on going back to the souvenir stalls, and since it was getting late in the afternoon, Jarrett apparently decided not to protest.

Dinner that evening gave Hannah an oddly wistful sensation that took her by surprise. It was strange to sit at a table with a man and a small boy. She felt as if she were playing wife and mother. Most of the other guests in the hotel dining room undoubtedly assumed that the three were a family, and Jarrett and Danny did little to counteract the impression.

Hannah was amazed at Jarrett's willingness to talk with the child, letting the youngster chat eagerly about his experiences during the day. Danny, in turn, seemed quite happy to accept Jarrett in the role of substitute father for the evening.

"Can I watch TV?" Danny demanded as he polished off dessert. "One of my favorite shows is on tonight, and I haven't seen it since we left home."

"I think that can be arranged," Jarrett agreed, glancing at Hannah with a smile. "Unless Hannah has other plans?"

"No, not really. I thought a walk on the beach might be nice after dinner, though. Would either of you be interested? I'm so stuffed after all those pineapple fritters!"

"I think that's a fair trade-off for a television show, don't you, Danny?" Jarrett inquired seriously.

"Sure. I can look for some more shells," Danny agreed enthusiastically.

"So can I," Hannah murmured, ignoring Jarrett's mocking eyes. What did she care if he didn't appreciate shells as souvenirs? The man was too wrapped up in ancient art for his own good.

It was still light out by the time the three of them had taken off their shoes on the beach and begun strolling along the waterline. Danny darted hither and yon searching out the best specimens, and Hannah wasn't far behind. She collected so many, in fact, that she wound up having to twist the skirt of her muu-muu into a makeshift sack. As eagerly as Danny, she hunted along the beach while Jarrett watched them both with a faintly indulgent expression.

"You're going to have to buy another suitcase to carry all those," he commented as she added another shell to her collection. "What are you going to do with them when you get home?"

"I think I'll decorate my plant containers with them," Hannah decided.

"Charming," he sighed.

"Here," she announced, holding out a large, tapering shell to him. "This one's for you. A souvenir of your little 'business trip' to the South Pacific." She regretted the impulsive gift almost immediately, and her chin came up with a touch of defiance as she waited for him to reject the shell.

Jarrett stared at it for a long moment until Danny came along and peered into his hand.

"That's a great one, Mr. Blade," the boy said enthusiastically. "If you don't want it, I'll take it."

"No," Jarrett said slowly, his eyes meeting Hannah's, "I think I'll keep it."

Hannah caught her lower lip between her teeth and gnawed on it for a moment, feeling strangely uneasy under his unreadable regard. "Of course, it's not as good a souvenir as that damn fertility goddess, but it won't cause you any legal trouble, either," she announced aggressively.

"What's a fertility goddess?" Danny demanded before Jarrett could respond.

That got to Hannah's sense of humor. "Go ahead, Jarrett, explain it to the boy," she said with a grin and then went off in search of more shells.

Hannah had half expected Jarrett to retreat to his own room once they returned to the hotel, but he didn't. He endured what passed for prime time television together with Hannah and only began glancing at his watch as ten o'clock approached.

"Aren't you getting sleepy, Danny?"

"Nope. I never get to stay up this late at home!"

"I'll bet," Jarrett said dryly. "When are his parents due back, Hannah?"

She frowned. "I don't know. I didn't put them under a schedule!"

Jarrett's eyes darkened, but he said nothing. Danny eventually went to sleep in the middle of Hannah's bed, and she turned down the television. Its tube continued to flicker through the room, and in the ghostly glow she glanced at Jarrett, who was sitting beside her.

He reached out and caught her hand, saying nothing. But his eyes never left hers as he drew her fingers slowly to his lips.

"Jarrett, please don't," she whispered anxiously, trying to retrieve her fingers.

"Quiet, or you'll wake Danny." Deliberately he kissed each fingertip. She felt his warm breath on her palm; then he turned over her wrist and kissed the sensitive skin there. "You still smell a little like suntan lotion. I wanted to help you put that lotion on today, Hannah. I wanted to have an excuse to touch you. There's something very intriguing about you."

"E-even if I do have lousy taste in souvenirs?" she tried to say lightly. She knew it didn't quite come off. The whole situation was about to get out of hand, and she should be taking steps to control it before Jarrett did the controlling for her. The easiest thing would be to "accidentally" awaken Danny and let him play chaperone. If she could keep him awake!

"You might have lousy taste in art, but I think you yourself will taste very good," Jarrett murmured. His tongue touched the inside of her forearm experimentally.

"Jarrett, stop that. What's the point of seducing me? I'm already doing everything you want me to do, aren't I? I let you set up poor Alice Clydemore this morning. What more do you want?"

"You," he said simply. "I've been wanting you all day, Hannah."

"You just want to seduce me because it will make you feel even more in control of me," she protested violently.

"Can a man control you with sex, Hannah?" he whispered starkly. His eyes burned suddenly into hers. "Would you give yourself so completely to a man that he could actually control you that way?"

She gasped, frantically trying to yank her arm back. "I'm certainly not about to let you experiment and find out!" Something told her that going to bed with Jarrett Blade would be the riskiest thing she had ever done in her life.

With unerring, primitive feminine instinct, Hannah prepared herself to draw away from the man beside her. She freed her hand with an abrupt movement and jumped to her feet, eyes wide and heart beginning to race.

"Leave me alone, Jarrett Blade. Don't touch me!"

"You're really afraid of me, aren't you?" he asked in a surprised tone. "There's only one reason for that, Hannah..."

She was about to silence him with a wild protest when a knock sounded on her door. Feeling as if a life preserver had just been thrown to her while she struggled in deep water, Hannah ran to the door and flung it open.

"Hi. We're a little late." Annie Tyler smiled apologetically. "Is Danny asleep?"

"Yes, yes he is," Hannah said quickly, vividly aware of Jarrett coming up behind her. He had the sleeping boy in his arms, and he handed him over to his father.

"A nice kid," Jarrett said coolly. "But I'm afraid Hannah won't be able to do any more baby-sitting. She's going to be busy for the remainder of her trip."

Ralph Tyler nodded quickly. "Sure, I understand. We really appreciate all you've done for us, Hannah."

Annie Tyler didn't look quite so enthusiastic over the prospect of losing the free baby-sitter, but she had the grace to smile and nod agreeably. "You've been great with Danny. He'll miss you."

"Oh, he's welcome to—"

"No, I'm afraid he's not welcome. Not in the evenings," Jarrett cut in smoothly. "The hotel offers a baby-sitting service, though. Perhaps you'd like to look into that."

Annie flushed. "Of course. It's just that Danny doesn't like strangers, and..."

"Come on, Annie, it's late." Ralph Tyler nodded down the hall in the direction of their hotel room. "Good night, Hannah, and thanks again. We'll see you in the morning."

"Good night," Hannah said with a touch of desperation as Jarrett firmly closed the door. Then she took refuge in her temper. "Honestly, Jarrett, you had no right to be so rude to the Tylers! I was perfectly happy looking after Danny. It's not as if they asked me to baby-sit him every night or anything, and I..."

"Honey, they were using you. They should never have asked you to baby-sit in the first place. You're on vacation too! And hotels the size of this one always have baby-sitting services available."

"You don't know what you're talking about!" she fumed.

Jarrett reached out and caught her defiant chin in his hand. "Hannah, let's get something straight," he said a little roughly. "If anyone's going to take advantage of you, it's going to be me!"

His mouth came down on hers with such dominating intensity that she stumbled against him. An instant later she was locked in his arms.

Four

It was like being caught up in a whirlwind. Hannah wanted to free herself and couldn't think of any way to do it. She couldn't really think at all, not with Jarrett's mouth controlling hers with a sensual command unlike anything she had ever experienced. Hannah found herself clinging when she knew she should have been pushing herself away from the intense demand of his body.

"Hannah, honey," Jarrett muttered against her lips, "I'm going to take you tonight. I'm going to lay you down and find out just how soft and warm you really are. Don't fight me, sweet Hannah, just give yourself to me and I'll take care of you. I'll make you happy tonight, I swear it."

His words continued to pour over her like warm honey, sweet and tantalizing and full of masculine promise. Hannah shivered beneath them, fiercely aware of a wild new recklessness moving within her.

On one level she was frightened of this man, but on another she was inexplicably drawn to him. From the first moment that she had allowed herself to fantasize about him aboard the plane, she had been aware of him in a way that was entirely new to her.

Now he had declared that he wanted her. The wild fantasy in which she had indulged had come true. The attraction was there, waiting to be acted upon. All she had to do was surrender....

But surrender was a dangerous thing to give Jarrett Blade. It was exactly what he wanted, but what would he do with it when he had it? How would he use it against her? It was too risky by far to even contemplate giving herself to this man. He was quite capable of taking the gift, *but what would he do with it?*

"Leave everything to me, Hannah. I want to learn all there is to know about your softness. I'll take care of everything."

Then his mouth closed on hers again, his tongue pushing warmly between the barrier of her teeth as he began to explore the prize he intended to take completely.

It was her chance, Hannah told herself, her one chance in a lifetime to learn the nature of passion and sensual excitement. Once before she had given herself in lovemaking to a man who had no respect for her or desire for love. The experience had been a disaster, leaving her crushed and unfulfilled and alone.

She had never been tempted to repeat it until tonight.

But tonight she would have an element of safety, Hannah assured herself as her arms stole around Jarrett's neck. Tonight there was no possibility that she was in love. How could there be? She had only known him a couple of days, and he had hardly been courting her during that time!

Jarrett Blade would probably be incapable of courting any woman, Hannah thought fleetingly. He had no use for gentleness or tender persuasion. He would not make himself vulnerable to a woman.

And this was the man with whom she was contemplating a brief vacation affair? But his very lack of loving desire was one of the elements which gave her safety, Hannah tried to tell herself. He would make no emotional demands on her, and she could keep her heart free even as she indulged her crazy fantasy.

"Oh, Jarrett, it's all so confusing," she whispered into his shirt as he lifted his mouth from hers. Unable to meet his eyes, she clung to him, trembling.

"No, it's not," he growled huskily, his hands roaming down her back to the curve of her hip. "Between you and me it's all very simple. I want you tonight and I think you want me. Relax, honey, and let it happen."

"But there's no love between us," Hannah said bleakly, her words muffled by his shirt. She felt his hands tighten on her waist.

"Don't you think you could learn to love me tonight?" he asked deeply. "Just a little, Hannah?"

Startled that he should even want such a response from her, Hannah's head came up sharply and her wide, anxious eyes searched his gaze. "Is that what you want, Jarrett? Really?"

"I want you completely. If you have love to give, even a little, then I want that, too."

She shivered, unable to comprehend the meaning behind his words. Dare she take them at face value? "It's so dangerous, Jarrett." *For me.*

"Not if you're honest with me, honey. Not if you surrender with no ulterior motives. I'll be as honest with you as you are with me. Fair enough?"

"It sounds crazy. All wrong somehow. Jarrett, I don't understand you or myself tonight."

"You don't have to understand. Leave everything to me," he soothed. Then he gently twined his fingers into the coiled braid of her hair and pushed her face against his chest so that she could not speak.

Oh, God, she wanted him, Hannah thought over and over again. She wanted him in a way that was so new to her. His fingers began to loosen the coronet of twisted hair and she heard his soft sigh of pleasure when the fine mass of cognac-brown came free in his hands, cascading down her back.

"I knew it," Jarrett rasped softly against her throat as he tangled his hands in her hair. "You don't really belong in the twentieth century at all, do you? With your hair down like this you look as if you stepped out of another world. And when I have you completely naked in my arms I think you are going to seem even more primitive."

Hannah took a deep breath, aware of how significant the act of taking down her hair had been. It left her feeling as if he'd already moved to claim her, as if he'd exerted a right over her that she hadn't been aware of giving him.

Dangerous. Primitive and dangerous. And irresistible.

With a sigh of surrender, Hannah let her body soften against Jarrett's lean strength. This was what she wanted, regardless of what the morning brought in the way of regrets. Tonight she would let herself experience the mystery that was Jarrett Blade.

"Sweet Hannah," he growled, sensing her unspoken surrender. "There's nothing left to think about tonight. Just let yourself feel. Just give yourself to me." He held her a little distance away, intently searching her face for a long moment.

Wordlessly she returned his searching gaze, knowing her growing desire must be showing in her eyes. Then he moved a hand from her waist and deliberately fitted it to her breast. Another small act of possession, she realized, just as taking down her hair had been. Was that what making love with Jarrett would be like? Nothing more than being possessed?

"Jarrett..."

He lifted his hand from her breast to lightly touch her lips. "No more words, honey. We've both made our decisions."

Then he bent to lift her into his arms, striding effortlessly through the connecting door. Hannah found herself being set down on a bed that had already been turned back, and the first thing she saw was the golden statue of the ancient fertility goddess on the nightstand.

"I took her out of hiding earlier when I turned back the bed," Jarrett said quietly as his eyes followed hers. "Something about her makes me think of you."

Before Hannah could respond he was sitting down on the bed beside her, his fingers finding the fastening of the muu-muu she was wearing. Hannah sucked in her breath as he deliberately lifted the dress from her body, leaving her in only a small bra and matching panties.

"Round and soft and womanly," Jarrett breathed, gray eyes gleaming in the shadows as he let his hand glide up her thigh to her stomach. "You were made for making love and making babies."

Hannah shook her head even as her body responded to his touch. "I'm not sure I like the sound of that. A bit limited as careers go." She tried to keep the words light in an attempt to ward off the certainty in his voice.

He didn't smile. Instead his expression became even more intent. "A thousand years ago you wouldn't have needed any other career."

"Jarrett, I think you're the one living in the wrong century," Hannah whispered as she touched his shoulder. A tiny smile curved her mouth and her eyes were soft and inviting in the pale light of the tropical moon.

"I think you may be right," he agreed huskily. Then his fingers freed the catch of the bra. Instantly the banked fires in his eyes flamed into full, glorious life. His palm grazed across one nipple as he bent down to kiss her. "Come alive for me tonight, Hannah. Let me have all you can give."

She cried out softly as her breast seemed to tighten and swell beneath his touch. His palm moved back and forth until the nipple firmed. In a small, convulsive spasm of mounting excitement, Hannah's leg flexed.

"Oh, Jarrett!" Fumbling, her fingers groped for the buttons of his shirt. She felt him tense as she began to free him of the garment. Then he pulled away.

Rising to his feet, Jarrett finished undressing himself in the shadows, peeling off the shirt and unclasping the belt of his slacks. In a moment or two he was naked in the moonlight, his body proudly, fiercely, aroused.

Hannah stared up at him, a little fearful now of the masculine power which was about to overwhelm her. He must have seen the uncertainty in her face, because he came down beside her with muttered words of reassurance and command.

"It's too late to change your mind, honey. You want me and you know it. Stop thinking about it." He flattened his hand on her stomach and then eased his fingers beneath the elasticized edge of her panties. He felt Hannah stiffen momentarily as the final barrier was breached and he folded his hand warmly against the melting core of her femininity. "Far too late to change your mind," he repeated with deep satisfaction. "Your body would betray you if you tried."

It was true. Hannah whimpered softly with desire, turning her face into his shoulder. Never had she been at the mercy of her own passion before. The experience was heady and frightening, and it left her breathless. Wonderingly she inhaled the intoxicating scent of Jarrett's body, her hand slipping down his chest to shape the hard line of his hip.

"Do you like the feel of me?" He caught her trailing hand and moved it to his thigh. "Touch me, Hannah." Deliberately he moved her trembling fingers to the thrusting evidence of his manhood.

"You seem so...so strong," she whispered. "Jarrett, you frighten me a little."

"A little fear won't hurt. And it will soon be gone," he assured her.

Slowly, deliberately, he stroked her body into full arousal. Never had Hannah guessed she was capable of such burning desire. It seemed to engulf her, causing her legs to twine with Jarrett's and her hands to pull at him. She wanted him to quench the fire that had begun to rage inside her. Instinctively she pressed herself closer, enticing him with the ancient wiles of womanhood.

But Jarrett refused to be pulled too quickly into the vortex of the passion he was creating. Slowly it dawned on Hannah that he was determined to set the pace. It was as if he meant her to know that even in this he would be the one in command.

"Jarrett, oh, Jarrett, *please!*" she begged, clinging to him as he rained kisses across her full breasts. "I need you."

"I know," he breathed triumphantly. "I can feel your need."

But he would not satisfy it completely. Instead he drew patterns in the soft hair at the juncture of her legs while he nipped gently at the tight buds of her nipples. His heavy leg pushed between her soft thighs, the roughness of it sending thrills along her nerves. Hannah was soon a twisting, curling bundle of aching feminine desire.

Yet when she could stand the sensual tension no longer and tried to push him onto his back so that she herself could complete the union, Jarrett caught her wrists and pinned her back against the mattress.

"No," he vowed, gunmetal eyes blazing with his own fiercely checked desire, "not yet."

"Oh, Jarrett, I can't stand it any longer!"

His mouth curved faintly in satisfaction. "I like you this way, Hannah. You're all woman and you're all mine, aren't you?"

She didn't know what he meant, but if it would serve to hurry him toward the shimmering conclusion of this encounter, she would agree with anything he said. "Yes, Jarrett. Yes! Please take me now. I'm going out of my head. I've never felt like this!"

Slowly, as if he would savor every second of the joining, Jarrett lowered himself along the length of her body. "Put your legs around me," he groaned.

Willingly she did as he commanded, although obeying him left her feeling more physically vulnerable than she had ever felt in her life. Eyes squeezed shut, she clung to him. Then he was pushing against her, probing slowly.

Hannah gasped as she felt the full extent of his masculine strength at the gate of her passion. And although she ached for him as she had never ached for a man in her life, Hannah was suddenly gripped with a wholly unexpected tension.

Jarrett must have felt it immediately. He paused, and when she opened her eyes he was lying very still, watching her. For a long moment they stared at each other.

Jarrett's expression was rigid with sensual intent, his eyes like molten silver in the moonlight. "It's all right, Hannah," he ground out carefully. "Relax. Give yourself to me."

"Jarrett, I'm afraid," she confessed in a tiny, ragged voice.

"I can taste your fear," he whispered, bending to run the tip of his tongue along her parted lips. "It's because you don't know where it will all end. You don't know how much of you I'll take. But I've already told you, sweetheart, I'm going to take all you have to give."

He waited no longer, entering her with a slow, firm power that made Hannah's breath catch in her throat. She closed her eyes tightly once more, her fingers clenching into the muscles of his back. Her body shivered in response to the steady, deliberate invasion and then it welcomed the invader completely.

"Ah, Hannah!" Her name was a throaty cry of triumph as Jarrett reacted to the acceptance of his body by hers. He began to move, driving into her with steady, pulsing strokes that sent Hannah into a whirling, spiraling climb.

Nothing else mattered except this moment and this man. Nothing else in the whole world. The little fertility goddess on the nightstand gleamed in the moonlight as Hannah learned the full extent of her own sensuality. When the pulsating climax gripped her, sending wave after wave of convulsive ripples into the deepest regions of her body, Hannah gave herself up to it completely. And in the process she gave herself up to the man who had commanded such an incredible response from her.

Jarrett took her gift with savage delight, his own cry of satisfaction a hoarse shout muffled against her breast.

Long moments later Jarrett stirred slowly, lifting his head to look down into Hannah's love-softened face. She could feel the cooling perspiration on his body as well as her own as reality filtered back.

"We have a lot to talk about in the morning, honey," Jarrett whispered huskily.

"Do we?" Hannah looked up into the face of the man to whom she was very much afraid she had just given her heart. Hope flared in her breast.

"Yes, but it can all wait until morning. God! I feel so good right now." Jarrett stretched luxuriously, keeping her body covered with his own. "So good."

Hannah smiled tremulously. "So do I. I've never felt anything like that before in my life, Jarrett," she confessed softly.

"Are you still frightened of me?"

Was she? she asked herself. "I don't know you very well. In fact, I can hardly believe I'm lying here with you tonight. I know so little about you, Jarrett." It was a plea for communication, for reassurance. It came from her heart.

"You'll be safe with me as long as you're honest with me," he told her quietly.

"Honest with you?" Bewildered, Hannah tried to read his eyes.

"I think you will be now, won't you, honey?" Jarrett drawled with easy certainty as he rolled off her and onto his back in a satisfied sprawl. "Tell me about your relationship with the Clydemores, Hannah. The whole truth."

"The Clydemores!"

"Are you working with them?" He turned his head to pin her with his gaze.

"Jarrett, I've already told you everything I know. Why bring it up now?"

"Because now I'm sure you can't lie to me," he said simply. His eyes held such masculine assurance that Hannah wanted to claw at them.

"Now you're sure!" The beginnings of dismay and shock brought Hannah to a sitting position, her gaze darkening as she stared down at him. Hastily she clutched the sheet to her breast, suddenly very conscious of her nakedness. "Was that what this was all about, Jarrett? Was making love to me some sort of bizarre test?"

The brackets around his mouth tightened, but he kept his voice calm and even. "You told me a lot by the way you made love. I don't think you realized just how much you revealed about yourself."

A flame of seething, purely feminine anger began to burn deep in Hannah's soul. She stared at the man lying at his ease beside her. "I don't believe this!"

"Tell me about the Clydemores, Hannah," he ordered softly.

Hannah's eyes narrowed as she succumbed to her fury. "You want to know about the Clydemores? Okay, I'll tell you about them. I'm working with them. We set you up with that damn fertility goddess! She's a fake, Jarrett! A fake, do you hear me? We knew you'd come out of the woodwork to get her back for your friend and in the process try to seduce me. I'm going to pretend to be so mesmerized by your phenomenal sexual talents that you'll want a full-scale affair with me. Once I'm in your home, I'm going to be able to rip off your entire pre-Columbian collection. The Clydemores are going to market it and split the profits with me! There! How's that for a grand scheme! Does that suit your distrusting, paranoid view of reality and of women?"

"Hannah, stop it," he gritted as she scrambled off the bed, taking the bedspread with her to cover herself. "Come back here and stop acting like a child. You just told me the sex was good for you. Why are you so mad?"

She whirled beside the bed, her breasts heaving with the force of her anger. Aqua eyes flashed with blue fire. "The sex might have been good, but it wasn't anywhere good enough, you bastard. I want a man who can give a little of himself while he's taking from me, but you can't do that, can you?"

"Now calm down and listen to me. And forget about that wild tale you just told me. I know damn well you made it up on the spur of the moment. Just tell me the truth."

"The truth," Hannah gasped, seizing the golden goddess in both hands and raising it high over her head, "is that I never want to see you or this stupid goddess again!"

"Hannah!" Clearly horrified by the prospect of her hurling the goddess halfway across the room, Jarrett leaped from the bed. "Give me that. Don't you dare throw it at the wall! It's priceless!"

"Then I'll throw it at you!" She slung the rounded figure at him, heedless of whether or not he had time to catch it. He managed, just barely, but Hannah didn't stick around for another attempt. She fled, naked, from the room. As she passed through the open connecting door, she shoved wildly at it, slamming it closed and locking it in one swift motion. She was almost unable to see what she was doing because of the burning tears filling her eyes.

Dashing the back of her hands across her eyes, Hannah fled into the bathroom and turned on the shower full force. She needed a bath. Nothing made a woman feel so unclean as when a man used her.

"Hannah!" The shower curtain was shoved aside to reveal Jarrett. The key to the connecting door was the only thing he was wearing. He tossed it down on the sink and confronted her with his hands on his lean hips.

"Get out of here, Jarrett. I'm taking a shower. I want to get rid of the feel of you!"

He smiled grimly. "You'll never succeed in doing that." Then he glanced at the wet strands cascading down her back. "You're going to have to sleep on wet hair. Why didn't you put on a shower cap?"

"The wet hair is my problem. Leave me alone."

"It's my problem, too, since you'll be sleeping with me," he told her evenly, stepping into the shower with her.

Hannah backed against the tile wall, holding up her hands as if to ward him off. "Jarrett, I'm warning you..."

He captured her hands and pulled her against his body, a faint smile touching his mouth. "Just tell me the truth about the Clydemores."

"I've already told you the truth!" she cried, frantically trying to free herself.

"You know them only as fellow tourists? You had nothing to do with stealing that statue?"

"No, I had nothing to do with it! But why ask me? You're going to believe exactly what you want to believe anyway!"

"I believe you now," he said gently, stroking his hands along her back beneath the curtain of her hair. "You really can't lie, can you? I was almost sure of it because of your eyes. But now I'm positive. In my arms you give me everything, including the truth. I think you gave me some love, too, didn't you, sweetheart? That's why you're so angry at the moment. But you don't have to worry. I'm not going to throw it back in your face."

She blinked uncomprehendingly. "What are you saying? That you...that you love me a little, too, Jarrett?" Her heart beat erratically as she waited tensely for his response. She could tolerate almost anything from him, even his ancient philosophy on how to handle a woman if he actually loved her. Philosophies could be changed, but the existence of love or the lack of it was another matter.

"I didn't say that, sweetheart," he murmured. He continued to stroke her back as if she were a high-strung mare. "I said I wouldn't throw your love back in your face. I'll take good care of it and of you, Hannah. You won't have cause to regret loving me."

"I regret it already! My God, Jarrett, I want a man who knows how to love, not one who just knows how to take that emotion from a woman!"

"Love is a woman's emotion, honey," he soothed. "It suits you. It makes you even softer and warmer than you already are. But a man who is in love is weakened by it. And there's no surer way for a man to lose his woman than to have her discover that he's weak. I won't let you make me weak, Hannah. But rest assured that I'll only use my strength to protect you and take care of you. That's what a woman needs from a man: strength and protection. All I demand of you in return is honesty and loyalty."

"Oh, is that all?" she quipped angrily, unable to believe what she was hearing.

The corner of his mouth kicked up whimsically. "Well, maybe not all."

"Do go on, I don't want to miss anything on the list! What else am I expected to provide in exchange for your masculine strength and protection?"

"The love and affection you need to bestow on a man, for starters," he suggested softly. "It's there inside you, honey, and you have to give it to someone."

Her chin tilted defiantly. "I get it. I'm supposed to love, honor, and obey and in return you're willing to provide nothing!"

The amusement faded from his eyes. "I'll keep my part of the bargain."

"But I don't happen to need what you're offering. This is the modern age, Jarrett. Raw strength doesn't come in very handy in an era of computers. As for protection, I pay my taxes like everyone else, and one of the things the money buys is a police force. Do I make myself clear? I don't need what you're offering! I'll save my love for a man who knows how to return it! Why are we even discussing the matter? You act as if there were some future for us, and you know damn well there isn't. This is what's known as a vacation affair."

Jarrett's hands went to her shoulders as his eyes hardened. Water cascaded down his chest, making him glisten. "You know as well as I do that what we just had together isn't going to end when you go back to Seattle."

"How do I know that?" she stormed. But she did know it, and the knowledge was terrifying in its implications. She would never be totally free of this man now that he had claimed her.

He shook his head, his eyes suddenly gentle. "I can see you're as aware of the future as I am. I've waited a long time to find a woman I can trust, Hannah, and I'm not about to let her go now that I've found her."

She looked up at him helplessly, feeling as if she were caught in a deep patch of quicksand. "What do I have to do to prove you can't trust me?"

"Well, you'll have to do better than that story about a fake fertility goddess and a plot to steal my collection." He grinned, leaning down to brush his lips across her nose. "But, frankly, you haven't got much of a chance. I told you last night I didn't think you could lie very well. Tonight I'm sure you can't."

"I did okay lying to Alice Clydemore today! I can lie just like anyone else!"

"I didn't say you couldn't try to lie, I merely said I'd always know if you were making the attempt. Alice Clydemore was probably much too rattled about losing the goddess to waste time studying your eyes. If she had, she would have seen the uneasiness you were radiating. Or perhaps she wouldn't have seen it," Jarrett decided musingly. "Maybe I'm the only one who really understands you."

"You don't begin to understand me," Hannah wailed helplessly.

He shook his head. "Something about you attracted me the moment I saw you on the plane, even before I decided you might be working for the Clydemores. Yesterday I spent hours watching you, studying you..."

"You didn't!" She was honestly shocked.

"I did. Why does that surprise you? After all, I had to know where you fit into the scheme of things. And I liked watching you. Even if you hadn't been involved with the Clydemores, matters would have ended the same way between us. I want you, Hannah. You're soft and gentle and there's something so deeply feminine about you..."

"That's a ridiculous thing to say," she squeaked, stunned by the insistent urgency in his words. It frightened her all over again. "All women are feminine by definition."

"No, not all. Some are as hard and cold and ruthless as any man when it comes to getting what they want."

"And you don't think I could be?" she demanded furiously.

Jarrett smiled again, his mouth a curve of certainty and satisfaction. "If anything, you're not hard and tough enough. Look at the way the Clydemores used you. And the way the Tylers took advantage of you as a free baby-sitter. My guess is those two instances are probably indicative of the way you live your whole life. How did you lose your job in Seattle, honey?"

She stiffened, alarmed at his flash of perception. "I got laid off. There was a reduction in the work force due to the economic situation, and I..."

He bent to shush the flow of words with his mouth. Then he lifted his head again. "You're lying. See how easily I can tell?" he asked tenderly. "Tell me the truth. Did you lose your job because you were the weak one in a power struggle? Or because someone used you some-how?" He gave her a small shake. "Tell me, Hannah. I want to know if I'm right. Did your innate softness get you into trouble?''

Hannah glared up at him. ''Well, you can just keep wondering. I'm not about to discuss my entire personal life with you just because you're curious to know if you're right!''

Which he was, she thought dismally. How had he guessed? Was he really able to read her so well? Had he really been able to draw such conclusions about her based on knowing her for only a couple of days. It was unnerving and very unsettling. She felt far too vulnerable around this man, both physically and emotionally.

''I'm not going to push you about it tonight, honey, so you can relax,'' Jarrett assured her as if he genuinely wanted to soothe the rising turmoil in her. ''You can tell me about how you lost your job some other time.''

''Don't hold your breath,'' she muttered fiercely.

''I'd rather hold you.'' He pulled her closer against his water-slick body, letting her know the returning sensual power in him.

''Let me go!'' Hannah began to struggle with the wild, useless, frantic fluttering of a small, trapped bird. ''Jarrett, please let me go!''

To her surprise, he released her. But his voice was stern when he spoke. ''Hannah, calm down. There's no need to have hysterics about this.''

''Why not? It's part of my deeply feminine, soft, weak personality!'' she yelped, shoving at his chest. ''If I want to have hysterics in the shower, I'll have hysterics!''

He frowned. ''It's obvious you're not in any condition to be rational about the situation tonight.''

''How perceptive of you!''

''So I'll leave you alone. Go to bed, Hannah. We'll talk this over in the morning when you've had a chance to calm down.'' He stepped out of the shower, grabbed one of the towels from the rack, and turned to glance over his shoulder as he started out the door. "If you get lonely between now and morning, honey, you're welcome to come back to my bed."

"Gosh, thanks," she gritted scathingly. "Your generosity overwhelms me! I'd advise you not to stay awake waiting for me, though. I'm going to try to be real strong and tough and make it through the night all by myself!"

"Sarcasm doesn't become you, Hannah."

Speechless at the overbearingly superior note in his voice, Hannah was unable to think of a fitting last word as Jarrett left the bathroom. When he had gone, she whirled around and turned off the shower. The wet length of her hair made her grimly aware of the fact that she was going to have to spend the next half hour with the blow dryer. Stupid. Why hadn't she thought to put it under a shower cap as Jarrett had suggested?

Because she hadn't been thinking at all when she'd fled his bed. She'd reacted with the emotional side of her nature instead of the intellectual side. But, then, if she'd been acting intelligently she never would have allowed herself to be seduced by that damn chauvinist in the first place!

What an idiotic way to wind up an expensive vacation. Miserably Hannah plugged in the blow dryer and began the long process of drying her wet hair. How had she ever gotten into such a humiliating mess?

Since her painful experience with Ned Ferris the year after she'd graduated from college, she had been so careful of involvement. She'd had male friends, but she had never allowed them to become lovers.

But all the while she had been protecting herself from shallow relationships, she had been longing for the real thing. A part of her would never stop seeking the love and commitment she needed to give and to receive. Long ago Hannah had made up her mind to wait until she found the right man before she again risked her heart. Until tonight it had been surprisingly easy to resist the overtures of the men she knew. For four years she had been content with casual dating relationships.

How could she have let everything go to pieces tonight? And with a man like Jarrett Blade, of all people.

"If you were going to have a vacation fling, why didn't you at least pick someone handsome and charming and polite?" she demanded of herself in the mirror. "Why did you have to pick a dangerous, uncharming bastard like Jarrett Blade?"

How had he slipped so easily past all her defenses? she wondered with a sad sigh. One thing was for certain. She had to leave as soon as possible in the morning. Hannah knew she couldn't risk another day of Jarrett's persistent company.

Willing herself not to give in to tears, Hannah turned out the light and climbed into bed, her hair still slightly damp. With any luck she would be safely back in her own bed tomorrow night.

The last image she had as she drifted off to sleep was of the rounded, golden body of the ancient fertility goddess crouching beside the bed during their dangerous voyage of sensual discovery.

A troubling realization hit Hannah just as she was about to surrender to sleep: She had been far too enthralled with the wonder of having Jarrett make love to her to worry about getting pregnant.

Surely she wouldn't...she *couldn't*...not by a man she had only known two days! A man who had thought her a smuggler and who had seduced her to satisfy his ego and his questions about her role in a theft!

Hannah lay awake a while longer trying to convince herself that over the centuries that damn goddess had lost her power.

Five

Hannah awoke with the suddenness that indicates underlying tension. It was barely dawn. As she sat up in bed and gazed out at the pearl-colored ocean, it occurred to her that it was indeed time to go home.

"One island morning is beginning to look a lot like another," she mumbled to herself as she pushed back the covers.

A quick glance at the connecting door assured her that the entrance to Jarrett's room was still closed. She winced as the memory of what had happened on the other side of that door the previous evening returned. Feeling depressed and uneasy, she began to dress quietly.

There was no point in trying to go back to sleep and it was far too early to have breakfast or call the airline company about changing her reservations. What she needed was an invigorating walk on the beach. At this hour she would have the long stretch of sand to herself.

There was no sound from Jarrett's room as Hannah pulled on one of her new flower-splashed muu-muus and slipped into a pair of sandals. Out of long habit she took the time to braid her hair and twist it into the familiar coronet. Maybe she'd cut it when she got back to the mainland. If it were very short she might forget the way Jarrett had wound his hands through it so possessively.

The crisp dawn air felt good and the beach was pleasantly deserted as Hannah made her way out through the hotel lobby to the waterfront. The sweep of Waikiki beach was ringed with elegant hotels, but they all looked curiously silent at this early hour.

She was tired, Hannah realized. The tour had been a grueling one, and she had been determined to take advantage of everything offered. Until last night the growing exhaustion had been rather pleasant, a sign of having enjoyed herself.

But this morning the tiredness had a depressing, restless aspect to it.

"Hannah!"

She turned at the familiar voice and found John and Alice Clydemore on the beach behind her. Surprised that they should be up so early, she paused and managed a smile. Their pace was brisk as they approached and the usual geniality seemed to be missing from their expressions. For the first time that morning Hannah suddenly found herself wishing the beach weren't quite so deserted.

She also found herself remembering something Jarrett had said about not knowing what the Clydemores might do when they discovered the statue was missing. But, then, she didn't really believe the Clydemores were guilty of the theft in the first place, did she?

"We saw you leave the hotel, Hannah," Alice began coolly as she and her husband came to a halt. The older woman's blue eyes were hard this morning, completely lacking in the usual warm charm Hannah had come to expect. "We've been waiting for a chance to see you alone. That Adams character who's been hanging around has monopolized you completely lately, hasn't he?"

"I don't know what you mean," Hannah began awkwardly, her mouth going dry just as her palms began to grow damp. There was no kidding herself now. The Clydemores were angry, which meant they must be guilty of having stolen that damned statue.

"Let's not beat around the bush," John Clydemore ordered flatly. "We want the statue back, Hannah. I don't know what kind of game you're playing or who you're working with, but it's over. The statue belongs to us."

"Then you shouldn't have let me run the risk of carrying it through U.S. Customs!" Hannah flared, deciding there was no point pretending ignorance now. What could they do to her here on the beach? Soon other people would begin filtering out of the hotels. As soon as someone else appeared, Hannah decided, she would call for help.

"I'm afraid we're becoming a bit too familiar to certain Customs officials," John Clydemore drawled. "Your naive, wholesome little face was exactly the sort we needed. I'll admit you had us fooled as well as Customs!"

"Who would have thought you were in the business?" Alice asked in tones of great disgust. "All that sweetness and light, taking care of the Tyler brat, buying all those junky souvenirs from every vendor with a sales pitch..."

"They aren't junky!"

Alice Clydemore ignored the interruption. "Gathering shells along every beach like a little kid, reading all those romances set in the South Seas as 'research,' helping every little old lady on the tour with her luggage and her problems. It's a hell of an act, Hannah, I'll give you that. Even had John and me fooled. But the game's over. Where's the statue?"

Hannah licked her lips and took a deep breath. A male figure dressed in khakis had emerged from the hotel entrance and was moving up the beach with a steady, strong stride. He was too far away to allow Hannah to see his features clearly, but there was something very familiar about his smooth, gliding pace. A sensation of relief swept through her. Jarrett was approaching.

"Mr. and Mrs. Clydemore," she began firmly, "I did not steal your stupid statue. I suggest you take the matter up with the gentleman who is coming toward us. I believe the three of you will have a lot to discuss, if I'm not mistaken. I, however, am not involved, so if you will excuse me..."

"Hold on, Hannah," John Clydemore said smoothly. "You're not going anywhere."

"Who's going to stop me?" she demanded, feeling more hostile than she had ever felt in her entire life. How dare all these people use her as a pawn in their smuggling games? "I've about had it with all three of you, do you hear me?" she went on aggressively as Jarrett came within listening distance. She sent him her most ferocious frown, a part of her thinking that this wasn't the most romantic "morning after" a woman had ever experienced. And it was all Jarrett's fault. "Jarrett, tell your friends here to leave me alone. You three can squabble about that damn statue as long as you like. But count me out!"

"That's exactly what we're going to do," Jarrett agreed easily. One dark brow arched in a gesture of command. "Go back to the hotel and wait for me, Hannah. I'll be along as soon as the Clydemores and I have sorted this out."

"Stop giving me orders!" Hannah yelped, even though going back to the hotel was exactly what she intended to do. "You should have been a drill sergeant, the way you're always giving orders!"

"Now see here, Adams, or Jarrett, or whatever your name is..." John Clydemore began, only to be interrupted by a glowering Hannah.

"His name is Jarrett. Jarrett Blade."

To her astonishment, that brought an immediate halt to Clydemore's words. Actually it brought a lot more than that, Hannah realized belatedly as the Clydemores turned to stare at Jarrett, who smiled sardonically. Alice had gone rather pale beneath her fashionable tan and John looked as if he'd been punched in the stomach. Breeding showed, however, Hannah admitted to herself. The Clydemores recovered quickly.

"Mr. Blade," John Clydemore said icily. "How interesting to meet you at last. I've heard of you, of course."

"And I've heard of you and your wife, Clydemore," Jarrett retorted. "Hannah, you can go now. I'll handle this."

Perversely Hannah stood her ground. "Actually, I'm getting a little curious. I think I'll stay for a while."

John Clydemore swung on her before Jarrett got a chance to issue another order. "So you're working with Blade here, is that it? That explains a lot."

"Like how a naive, scatterbrained tourist like myself could pull off the coup of stealing that statue?" Hannah returned sweetly, her eyes glittering with resentment.

"That's enough, Hannah," Jarrett cut in with a tone that did not encourage further defiance. "I told you to go back to the hotel. Move, woman."

For a moment longer Hannah debated the wisdom of ignoring him. The Clydemores were curiously silent, their attention on Jarrett. Jarrett concentrated the full force of his willpower on Hannah, and she found herself weakening. Jarrett Blade, she discovered, was not an easy man to defy. His gray eyes were hard and unyielding as he waited for her to obey.

"What in the world would make me want to hang around the three of you any longer than necessary?" Hannah asked rhetorically. Chin tilted regally, she took a few steps past the small group of intense people on the beach. They had their backs to her, but even so, she could hear John Clydemore's opening words to Jarrett.

"So, Mr. Blade. You couldn't resist taking the goddess for your own collection. I had heard you no longer operated in the international market. What made you decide to come out of retirement?"

"You made the mistake of taking the goddess from Jorge Valesquez's collection. Señor Valesquez is a friend of mine," Jarrett said quietly.

"And what will you tell your 'friend' when you are unable to return the goddess?" Alice Clydemore interjected sharply. "Because we all know that statue will never make it back to Señor Valesquez, don't we? It's going to disappear into the private collection of one Jarrett Blade."

Hannah didn't wait to hear anything else. She broke into a run and made her way swiftly back to the shelter of the hotel. It sounded as if Jarrett and the Clydemores understood each other very well. Was Jarrett really going to keep the statue for himself? Was he no better than the Clydemores?

Dammit! Why was she torturing herself with thoughts like that? It was obvious Jarrett Blade was in the same league as her ex-friends John and Alice. After all, if he'd been playing it straight, he would have called in U.S. Customs.

And she would have been in very hot water.

That last realization was a sobering one. Like it or not, she supposed she owed Jarrett some gratitude for not having turned her over to the authorities. But apparently the only reason he hadn't was that his own background was somewhat shady. So shady that the Clydemores automatically assumed he would keep the goddess for himself.

When she reached her room Hannah began throwing her belongings into a suitcase. Working frantically, she tried to stuff the Hawaiian souvenirs in with the others. If Jarrett hadn't destroyed a few of them that first night, she thought, she wouldn't have been able to get the shells into the bag. There wouldn't have been room. As it was, she'd have to carry the Maui potato chips on her lap.

A knock on her door came just a few moments before she was ready to leave. Hannah panicked and then realized that it had been a timid little knock. Not at all the kind of knock Jarrett Blade would use, if he bothered to knock at all. Nervously she answered.

"Oh, hi, Danny." She smiled in relief as she opened the door. "What are you doing here?"

"I came to see if you and Mr. Blade want to go swimming before breakfast. Mom and Dad said that if you did, I could go with you. They're still in bed," the boy added disgustedly. "They never want to do anything."

Hannah sighed. Poor Mom and Dad. They had wanted a second honeymoon. And poor Danny. He'd been dragged along on a trip that really hadn't been all that much fun for him. "Oh, Danny, I'm so sorry," she murmured, crouching in front of him and trying to smile. "I would love to take you swimming this morning, but I can't. I have to go home today."

Danny looked at her, perplexed. "I thought you'd be going home when we did. Why are you going early?"

"Because I have to." No point going into lengthy explanations with a kid, Hannah decided wryly. "I have lots of responsibilities at home. I've been away a long time."

He looked interested. "Have you got kids like me at home?"

"Well, no, but I do have some other creatures who will be missing me."

"Like what?"

"Let's see, there's Erasmus and Siegfried, Herbie, Yolanda and Ludmilla..."

"Those don't sound like kids!" Danny observed wonderingly.

"They're not. Erasmus is a dog and Siegfried is a bird. Herbie is a turtle and Yolanda and Ludmilla are a couple of plants. I have a few other plants, too. Want to hear their names?"

Danny shook his head. "I don't like plants much. But I like animals. I'd like Eras-rasmus and Sieg-whatever his name was. And Herbie, too. Maybe I could see them someday?"

"Maybe," Hannah agreed slowly, knowing what the odds were on that score. She got to her feet, ruffling Danny's light-colored hair affectionately. "Take care of yourself, Danny. It's been nice meeting you. I hope you enjoy school this fall."

"Good-bye, Hannah," the boy said wistfully. "Will Mr. Blade be going with you?"

"No, Danny. He won't." Hannah turned back into the room, took a last glance around, and picked up her overstuffed suitcases. "Could you close the door for me, Danny?"

"Sure." The boy obliged and then hesitated. "Want me to say good-bye to Mr. Blade for you?"

Hannah stiffened. "There's no need, thank you, Danny."

"But I think he likes you, Hannah," Danny objected.

"Mr. Blade likes his women with a little age on them," Hannah told him dryly. "Like a few centuries. Mr. Blade does not like me at all. He only wanted to use me for a while! Good-bye, Danny." Eyes burning with unshed tears, Hannah clutched her cases and hurried down the hall.

A good many hours later Hannah finally turned the key in the lock of the small house she rented in a friendly Seattle neighborhood. Instantly a cacophony of noise went up, a combination of welcoming barks and scolding squawks. It was good to be home.

"Erasmus!" Happily Hannah let go of her suitcases to go down on her knees in front of the large, enthusiastic dog that was doing his utmost to leap into her arms. Erasmus was really much too big to be leaping into anyone's arms, but he apparently still thought of himself as a puppy in some ways. His background might have been in doubt, but his joyous greeting was not. "You missed me!" Hannah exclaimed. "Did Jimmy remember to take you out twice every day? You don't look like you're starving. He must have remembered to feed you! How're Siegfried and Herbie?"

The squawking from the direction of the parakeet cage in the corner of the living room confirmed that Siegfried, too, had survived her vacation. The little yellow bird was racing back and forth on his perch, shrilly demanding attention. Herbie the turtle was a more staid creature by nature, not given to displays of affection, but even he stuck his head out to acknowledge Hannah's return. And Yolanda, Ludmilla, and the other plants all looked healthy and green.

By the time Hannah had greeted everyone, kicked off her shoes, and poured a glass of white wine for herself, she was feeling almost relaxed at last.

Almost, but not quite. Frowning at her drink while she absently scratched Erasmus's ears, Hannah considered her newfound restlessness. It would disappear in time, she promised herself. She would find another job soon and settle down into another routine that would be pleasant and satisfying.

After all, she liked her life the way it was, didn't she? Why should she be feeling so restless and uneasy? "Must be the vacation," she told Erasmus wisely. "There's always a letdown after a vacation, you know."

Erasmus snuffled intelligently and adjusted his head for a better scratching angle. He ignored the bird, which was hopping about in its cage beside the chair. He also ignored the turtle, which dozed happily on its island. He could afford to ignore them all because he was bigger than they were and he knew it.

Hannah glanced around her cozy living room, idly noting that everything looked much the same as when she had left ten days before. The hothouse window was filled with plants and herbs that had all stayed green with the help of a neighbor. The old-fashioned wingbacked chairs and pillow-covered sofa looked comfortable and inviting. The white area rug in front of the fireplace provided a pleasant focal point for the pastel color scheme of the room. Against the soft yellows and beiges, the green plants had a sculptured effect.

Hannah liked the house. She had been renting it for two years now, and it provided the backyard that Erasmus needed. But it wasn't cheap. She frowned at the thought.

"A lot of mouths to feed in here," she announced to the occupants of the room. "Looks like I'd better get cracking on finding another job."

There was silent agreement. No one else in the room was particularly worried, it seemed. Hannah smiled to herself. Dog, turtle, bird, and assorted plants were all blissfully content in the knowledge that they would be taken care of by her. They were, after all, the recipients of a deep and abiding affection. They had a home with Hannah.

Hannah finished her wine, notified her neighbor she was home a couple of days early, covered Siegfried's cage, and said good night to Herbie and Erasmus. Then she went to bed, exhausted. But her dreams that night were filled with dark fantasies of a man with somber brown hair and cold, lonely eyes. Lonely?

Yes, lonely, Hannah realized somewhere in the farthest recesses of her sleeping mind. Lonely. Jarrett Blade was a lonely, alienated man who would probably never learn what love was all about. At least she knew what it meant to love.

Hannah spent the next day unpacking and adjusting to being at home again. Regardless of how soothing it was to get back into her familiar routine, the restlessness did not fade. Would she always carry these annoying images of Jarrett Blade around in her head?

"I never even learned where he lived!" she complained to Herbie when she changed the water in his terrarium. "Not that I care. And you don't either," she added wryly as Herbie paddled blithely about, "do you? I suppose it doesn't matter to any of you that I had a mad fling while I was on vacation. That I actually let myself be seduced?" Hannah glanced at the dozing dog and the chattering parakeet. Neither bothered to respond. "How about the fact that I almost got myself arrested for smuggling? That news shake anyone here? No?"

Was it really a bad sign to find yourself carrying on extended conversations with pets and plants? No, Hannah decided resolutely, it was not.

As she arranged her collection of shells in Yolanda's and Ludmilla's pots, Hannah found herself remembering the evening she had gathered them. "I suppose he threw away the one I gave him," she confided to the rubber tree plant.

"He only likes treasures made of gold that have been buried for a thousand years."

Hannah postponed the evil task of job-hunting until a couple of days after her return. A glance into the eyes of her pets on the second morning convinced her she could put it off no longer. The extravagance of her trip to the South Pacific demanded that she find work soon now that she was home. She had used up a sizable portion of her savings on the tour. The little statue of King Kamahameha became a paperweight as she began overhauling her résumé. Every time she glanced at it she remembered Jarrett's mockery of the purchase.

"I hope he's home now enjoying his precious pre-Columbian artifacts," she told the cheap lava carving. "Old artifacts are about all he's capable of enjoying. And you know why? It's because they don't demand real love in return. The man doesn't know how to love." She frowned seriously at Siegfried, who was perched on the tip of her pen. "The funny part was that he had the nerve to tell me I was free to love *him*! I just wasn't supposed to expect anything in return! Talk about raw nerve! Oh, Lord. I really do have to find a job. I'm starting to talk to you and Erasmus and Herbie far too much."

"Love you. Love you. Love you," Siegfried chattered reassuringly.

The phone rang the next morning just as Hannah was licking her twentieth stamp and attaching it to the twentieth résumé-containing envelope. The voice on the other end of the line was cheerfully familiar. And pleasantly human.

"Charlotte! I'm so glad you called. How are things at the office?" Charlotte had been her co-worker in the information storage retrieval department of the large corporation where Hannah had worked. Together they had indexed and stored in a computer the countless documents, plans, and drawings produced by the manufacturing firm. The other woman was older than Hannah by about five years and married with three children. Hannah had missed hearing about the day-to-day adventures of the three Pomeroy kids.

"That's exactly why I'm calling," Charlotte announced grandly. "I'm so glad you're back. I couldn't remember exactly which day you were due to return. Have I got *news,* friend!"

"I'm sitting down." Hannah chuckled.

"You'd better be for this. Scoville got caught in a clinch with Jessica Martin in the supply room. Gossip is that Benson himself found them and this time he lost his temper."

"Benson found them?" Ronald J. Benson was the president of the company. "What on earth was he doing within fifty yards of a supply room? He never leaves the executive suite!"

"Hannah," Charlotte interrupted irritably, "you're seizing on the least important aspect of the situation. Apparently Benson's secretary was temporarily out of the office and he needed a new pen or something. Who cares why he happened to walk in when he did? The point is, he found them in a most compromising situation. And according to Harry Shaeffer, who happened to come along at just the right moment to hear *everything...*"

"Harry always did have a talent for overhearing *everything,*" Hannah observed.

"Well, the upshot of the whole thing was that Scoville has been asked to submit his resignation," Charlotte finished in triumph.

"You're kidding!"

"Nope. Knew that would get your attention. Benson reportedly told his vice-president that Scoville's name had cropped up one too many times in compromising circumstances and that this particular instance was the last straw. He wants Scoville out. By the end of the month.''

"Well, it's about time," Hannah murmured. "Jessica Martin, hmm? Poor kid. I'll bet she was devastated.''

"Didn't handle it nearly as well as you did," Charlotte giggled delightedly.

"I don't know about that. Has she still got her job?''

"Oh, yes. Benson didn't blame her at all. In fact, Hannah, now that the truth about Scoville's harassment is out, everyone's talking about how you should never have been let go. I'm positive you can get your old job back. I think you should phone Personnel today and reapply.''

"Do you really think so, Charlotte? it was all so horribly messy...''

"Listen, everyone knows now what kind of turkey Scoville was. Benson is a married man, remember? A happily married man. He expects a certain kind of behavior from his management staff. And he's setting the tone of office opinion. Everyone is firmly against Scoville now and in favor of the women who've complained about his harassment. Hannah, you need a job, right? Information storage and retrieval positions aren't exactly lying around on the ground right now. Please come back. I'd love to work with you again. We all miss you.''

"I'll think about it," Hannah offered slowly. After all, it had been a good job except for Doug Scoville's obnoxious advances. He had been her boss, and he had been accustomed to using his position to take advantage of any female employee who caught his eye. A few had cooperated willingly enough, it was true. Scoville was a handsome, self-assured man who promised much and delivered nothing. He was also a married man. Even if Hannah had wanted to believe his promises of advancement and love, she would never have allowed herself to become involved with a married man.

Scoville's persistent demands had become increasingly difficult to deal with. Personnel didn't want to have to confront him with accusations of harassment. He was too powerful, and many of the men in Personnel took the attitude that it was the fault of the women involved anyway. The situation had come to an embarrassing conclusion when Hannah was politely asked to leave.

"I hope you'll do more than think about it, Hannah. Believe me, things have really changed. Personnel got chewed out for not having paid attention to previous complaints about Scoville. Those guys will probably bend over backward to get you back on the staff."

"I'll give it some thought, Charlotte. Really. Now tell me, how are the kids?"

Charlotte laughed at the familiar question. "Oh, they're all running true to form. Scott fell out of the swings at day care yesterday and cut his arm. Had to rush him to Emergency. Corrie tried to find out if her pet goldfish can breathe air and Jimmy has a cold. Same old story. You haven't missed a thing. You know, Hannah, you ought to have some kids of your own. You're nearly thirty and you really shouldn't put it off much longer. I'm not sure it's healthy for you to be wasting all that love and affection on that menagerie and arboretum you maintain. Find yourself a nice man and have some kids, friend. Misery loves company."

"Gosh, thanks, Charlotte." Hannah laughed.

"Anytime, Hannah, anytime. Well, I've got to run. Mac McDonald is taking over this department until a replacement is found for Scoville. I've got to give him a rundown on how we operate. Promise me you'll reapply?"

"I promise. Good-bye, Charlotte. And thanks." Thoughtfully Hannah hung up the phone and reached for another envelope. She addressed it to the Personnel department of her old firm. Nothing to lose, and it had been a good job.

That evening she curled up after dinner with a novel—a spy thriller. Erasmus lounged on the rug in front of her and Siegfried played with his mirror. Herbie, as usual, wasn't terribly active, but he looked content investigating a shell Hannah had put in his terrarium.

Hannah was just coming to the conclusion of a particularly hair-raising chase sequence when the front doorbell chimed. Instantly Erasmus leaped to his feet, his shaggy body tense, ears cocked. He issued his standard warning bark and strode aggressively to the door ahead of his owner.

"Who is it?" Hannah called, her hand on the knob.

"It's Doug, Hannah. Let me in. I have to talk to you."

Hannah backed away from her side of the door as if it had grown alarmingly hot. Doug Scoville? Here at this hour? "What do you want?"

"Hannah, please let me in. I just found out you were back in town. We have to talk. I'm sorry about what happened. I came by to apologize for that incident at the office. That's the only reason I'm here, Hannah. I just want to say I'm sorry."

With a sigh of resignation and irritation, Hannah opened the door to reveal the good-looking man with the chestnut-brown hair and green eyes who had been directly responsible for causing her to lose her job.

It wasn't until she saw the strange glitter in his gaze and the too-steady way he held himself that she realized he'd been drinking.

Erasmus growled.

Six

By the time Jarrett had rented a car at Sea-Tac airport, found Interstate 5 into Seattle, and gotten lost three times after exiting the Interstate onto surface streets, he was not in the best of moods.

Damn town must have been laid out by a drunk, he decided, not knowing that local legend supported that theory. Eventually he found his way into the pleasant north Seattle suburb where the address he held seemed to fit the numbering system.

When he finally discovered the right block and the right house, it was after nine o'clock in the evening and even the late summer light had faded to deep dusk. Jarrett switched off the ignition and sat for a moment behind the wheel of the rented Chevrolet, staring at the warmly lit cottage.

The place looked like Hannah, he decided. The light seeping through the curtains had an inviting, golden quality. Somehow it reminded him of the cognac shade of her hair. There was a slightly overgrown but obviously cherished yard in front that seemed to extend around to the back of the house.

A garden would be nice, Jarrett was surprised to find himself thinking. He'd never bothered with one. But Hannah would look right at home planting seeds and picking vegetables. Yes, he'd have that terraced rockery at the back of his house torn out and replaced by a garden. She'd like that.

Thoughts of having Hannah safely established in his own home sent a ripple of anticipation through him. Jarrett's fingers tightened momentarily on the wheel, and then he drew a long breath. Why was he hesitating?

He'd come all this way just to find Hannah and take her back with him, and here he was sitting outside her house like a nervous high school kid trying to get up the nerve to pick up his first date.

There was nothing to be nervous about. Oh, sure, Hannah would probably put up a small battle, but it would be a token protest at best. All he had to do was start making love to her and she would melt in his arms. She might not even put either of them through that much trouble. After all, Jarrett reminded himself, she was half in love with him already. It wouldn't take much to secure her love completely.

It was a decidedly pleasant notion, the idea of being loved by Hannah Prescott. She would make a comfortable addition to both his home and his life. With a cool resolve, Jarrett opened the door and got out. Deliberately he headed toward the brick walk that led to the front door.

He would take good care of Hannah. She needed someone to shelter her, whether she realized it or not. He'd keep the Clydemores and the Tylers and Lord knew who else away from her. Hannah's sweet, naive nature led too many people to take advantage of her. He would protect her and give her a focus for all the warmth and passion she had locked inside. Jarrett had been telling himself he was the man to take care of Hannah ever since he had arrived back at his hotel room and found her gone. All the way home from Hawaii he had tantalized himself with pleasant pictures of Hannah in his home and in his bed.

It would be a good relationship for her. He'd see to it.

He was just about to sound the knock on the door when he caught the faint drone of a man's voice from inside the cottage. Jarrett frowned, glancing at the sleek Datsun sports car parked at the curb. Who the hell was visiting Hannah at this hour? Damn, he'd only given her a few days alone and already some creep in a snappy car was bothering her.

His frown intensifying, Jarrett rapped sharply on the door. Instantly a dog's loud, warning bark responded. The voices inside stilled. A moment later the door was flung open and Jarrett found himself staring hungrily down into Hannah's sweetly freckled face.

But there was no sign of welcome in the startled aqua eyes that lifted to meet his. In fact, he realized grimly, Hannah looked harassed and upset. And that could only be the fault of whoever was inside the cottage.

"Jarrett! My God! What on earth are you doing here?"

Dammit, she didn't have to look *that* astonished to see him. "I think the answer to that question is obvious. I came for you." Jarrett had fully intended to take her into his arms the moment he saw her again. But clearly other matters were going to have to come first. He clamped a hand around each of her nicely rounded shoulders, allowing himself an instant to savor the feel of her, and then firmly moved her aside. "What's going on in here, Hannah? You look upset." He pushed his way into the hall.

"Finding you at my door is not doing anything to improve my mood! Jarrett, please, I don't know why you're here, but I'm busy at the moment and I wish you would just go away.''

He ignored her request. She obviously was too agitated to realize what she was saying. Now was the time to be soothing but steadfast, he told himself. Dammit, he wasn't going to make any more mistakes handling Hannah. He'd learned his lesson the night he'd made love to her and then brought up the subject of the Clydemores. She was a romantic at heart, and a man would do well not to force the harsh realities of life on her.

"Honey, what's the matter? Is someone bothering you?"

"A couple of someones are bothering me!" she snapped irritably, "and they're both male. I wish I'd had the sense to send Erasmus to attack-dog school!"

"Erasmus? Oh, the dog. Hello, Erasmus." With the sure instinct of a man who'd never in his life owned a dog but who saw no reason why they shouldn't be dealt with rather like people, Jarrett put out his hand. Erasmus whimpered gently and thrust his damp nose politely into the extended palm. An instant bond was established, and Hannah glowered down at the dog.

"Men!"

"Honey, I don't know what's wrong, but whatever it is, I'll take care of it. Just tell me—"

"Hannah?" The interruption was caused by the masculine voice Jarrett had heard just before he'd knocked. "Hannah, what's going on? Who is this?" the stranger demanded as he moved into the hall behind Hannah.

Jarrett draped an arm around Hannah's shoulders with lazy possession, pulling her against his side. He paid no attention to the stiffness in her as he studied the other man. Good-looking but weak. The kind who would take advantage of a woman like Hannah. "I'm the one who should be asking the questions," Jarrett drawled. He felt

Hannah stiffen further, but he didn't release her. "Who the hell are you?"

The other man regarded him with a hint of aggression. "I'm a friend of Hannah's."

"Hannah's friends all have to be vetted by me, and I get the feeling I'm not going to approve of you."

"Jarrett, stop it!" Hannah struggled briefly within the curve of his arm, but he paid no attention. "Both of you cut it out this minute. I will not have my home turned into a back alley."

"Who is he, Hannah?"

"I'm Doug Scoville. I'm Hannah's boss."

"Not anymore," Hannah interjected quickly.

"Last I heard, Hannah had just lost her job," Jarrett murmured coolly. "If you were her boss, maybe you know something about that? Maybe you were responsible?"

"Now hold on just a minute, Mr...." Scoville began blusteringly.

"The name's Blade. Jarrett Blade. And I think that's about as close as our association is ever going to get. It's time you were gone, Scoville. Hop into that little car of yours and get lost."

"Dammit, I'm not going anywhere until Hannah and I have had a chance to talk. I don't know who you think you are, but..."

"I'm the man who looks after Hannah now. People like you will learn to stay away from her in the future," Jarrett explained calmly. "And I might as well tell you that you're only going to get one warning."

Hannah made another effort to extricate herself from the circle of his arm, but once again Jarrett ignored it. His hold wasn't enough to silence her tongue, however, and he heard the flare of temper in her words.

"If both of you don't stop acting like a couple of alley cats I'm going to scream until the police arrive, do you understand? I've had it with both of you. I want each of you to get into your car and leave, do you hear me? Just leave me alone!"

"Scoville, you're the one who's upset her like this," Jarrett gritted. "I don't allow other men to upset Hannah. Get out, before I throw you out."

"Dammit, you're not going to give me orders!"

Jarrett released Hannah and took a menacing step forward. He had no qualms at all about using force, and that fact must have shown. Scoville flinched, and then after an angry glance at Hannah's anxious face, he edged quickly toward the door. Erasmus barked good-bye, clearly glad to see him gone.

Jarrett moved to slam the front door shut just as Scoville gunned the accelerator of his Datsun. Then he turned to confront Hannah. "It's all right now, honey. He's gone." Soothing and gentle. That was the ticket now. He wouldn't give in to his own fury and demand a full explanation of Doug Scoville's presence in Hannah's home. With a great effort of will he told himself he would be tender and calming until Hannah relaxed and explained everything. No more mistakes, he vowed for the hundredth time.

"Well," Hannah began assertively as she faced him with her hands on her hips, "this is certainly turning into an eventful evening. What are you doing here, Jarrett?"

He eyed the way her sweet rear filled out her snug, faded jeans. There was a strong temptation to put out a hand and cup the soft shape, but Jarrett valiantly resisted. Nevertheless, the fullness of her breasts beneath the plaid shirt she was wearing and the roundness of her thighs brought back memories that he could hardly wait to relive. But he'd take this one step at a time.

"Stop glaring at me like that, honey," he muttered softly, stepping forward to assess the living room with an appreciative eye. "Your house looks just like you. Cozy and comfortable and inviting. Who's that?" He walked over to the birdcage and looked down at the yellow, feathered creature sitting on the swing.

"That's Siegfried. And I wish you would explain yourself, Jarrett. You had no right to barge in here and threaten my visitor." Hannah stormed into the room behind him just as Siegfried hopped onto Jarrett's extended finger. "Put him down. He bites."

"He'll only bite me once, won't you, Siegfried?" Jarrett traded stares with the bird for a moment.

"Don't you dare threaten my bird!"

"I'm not threatening him. We're coming to an understanding." Siegfried was apparently content with the "understanding," because after a moment's close assessment of the alien human on whose finger he was sitting, he calmly began to preen his already perfectly aligned feathers. Gently Jarrett deposited him back on his swing and glanced around. "Anyone else I should meet? Ah, here we go. A turtle. I'll bet he's a real comfort on a cold night, hmm? And look at all these plants. It looks as if you're trying to re-create the Amazon jungle in here. So! That's what happened to all those shells you collected, hmm?" He peered at the way they were artfully arranged in the various pots. "Wait until you see how the quilt looks in my bedroom."

"There's not a chance in hell I'll ever see how the quilt looks in your bedroom," Hannah sputtered in outrage.

He might as well lay his cards on the table. Jarrett straightened from studying the placid turtle and turned to face her, reminding himself to take it slow and gentle. "Of course you're going to see that Hawaiian quilt, honey. I've come to take you home with me."

She stared at him, her lips parted in astonishment. "Take me home with you!" she finally squeaked. "Are you out of your mind? I wouldn't go across the street with you."

"There's plenty of time to talk it all over," he assured her. "It's been a long trip. Have you got a drink?"

"No!"

"Are you sure? Scoville looked as if he'd had a couple." Jarrett heard the harshness creeping back into his voice and deliberately tried to suppress it.

"Doug had had a couple before he even showed up here tonight. Stay away from my kitchen, damn you!" She hurried after him as he walked into the other room.

With sound instinct Jarrett began exploring Hannah's kitchen. It was as cheerful and comfortable as the rest of the cottage. God, she was going to be pleasant to have around. Visions of his own home being turned into a cozy, warm environment flashed into his head just as he found the liquor cabinet.

"Jarrett, you have no right..."

Deftly he removed the whiskey bottle and located a couple of glasses. "Here you are." He handed her a glass with a small amount of whiskey and a large amount of ice and soda in it. Then he poured himself a rather large amount of whiskey over ice. "Take a few sips and calm down. We have a lot to talk about."

"I'm not in a conversational mood!" she warned vengefully as he pushed the glass into her hand.

"That's okay. I can do most of the talking." Taking her arm, he guided her back into the living room and pushed her gently onto the couch. She glared up at him and then took a long swallow of her drink. "If you hadn't run off that morning in Hawaii we could have had this little discussion then. And I wouldn't have had to chase after you like this."

"I'm terribly sorry you were put to so much trouble."

"I've told you before, honey, sarcasm doesn't become you. Now just settle down and listen." He ignored her outraged expression and plugged on determinedly, striving for a calm, controlled manner. "Hannah, it's obvious you need someone to look after you. You need a man."

"Oh, my God," she mumbled indistinctly, taking another swallow of whiskey.

"You're too soft and naive for your own good. Every time I see you, someone is trying to take advantage of you. The Clydemores used you to smuggle that goddess, the Tylers used you as a free baby-sitter, your ex-boss is clearly trying to get you into bed..." He broke off as a pink flush stained the cheekbones beneath her freckles. He knew he'd been close to the mark, but having this confirmation of it enraged him. It took a tremendous effort to control his temper. "Just what is the story with Doug Scoville? What happened to make you lose your job? And what was he doing here tonight?" Dammit, he'd intended to wait before he brought up that topic.

"It's none of your business," she informed him sullenly.

"You want me to track down Scoville and ask him?" Jarrett suggested far too mildly. He left no doubt in his tone that he'd do exactly that. The hint of menace was successful.

Hannah's lips tightened for a moment; then she attempted a cool little shrug.

"I'll tell you if it will speed up this 'discussion' we're having." She sighed. "Scoville was my boss. He had a nasty habit of sexually harassing the female employees who worked for him. I was one of the unlucky ones. He kept pestering me, making life very difficult on the job. I complained to Personnel, but they simply assumed it must be my fault. Scoville got worse after that, as if he knew he was safe. He was so sure..." She trailed off awkwardly, but Jarrett knew what came next.

"He tried to push you into an affair, and you refused." His fingers were like bands of steel around the whiskey glass now. He absently hoped it wouldn't fracture. It would be nice if the glass were Scoville's neck. He should have throttled the guy while he'd had the chance.

"It all came to a grand, humiliating conclusion the day he followed me home from work and tried to...to..." She licked her lower lip nervously.

"Tried to rape you?" Jarrett couldn't even feel the glass now. His eyes never left Hannah's face. All he could think about was going after Scoville.

Hannah made a wry expression. "I'm sure he thought of it as an attempted seduction," she muttered. "It, uh, failed. But Scoville's wife had become suspicious, apparently. She walked in just as things were getting very unpleasant. She was furious and blamed me. She then demanded that Scoville see to it I was fired. I resigned first. End of story. Satisfied?"

"Satisfied!" Jarrett exploded. "Are you crazy? I won't be satisfied until I take him apart piece by piece! Lady, you really do need a keeper, don't you? What the hell was he doing here tonight, as if I need to ask?"

"As long as you've obviously got it all reasoned out, why are you asking?" she snapped moodily.

"Because I want to hear all the gory details! I want you to spell it out so we'll both hear the words. Come on, Hannah, tell me exactly what he was doing here and then tell me you don't need me!"

"He came here to apologize," she said recklessly.

Jarrett grimaced, knowing at once that she was glossing over the truth. "Tell me exactly what sort of apology he wanted to make," he bit out. The little fool. Didn't she know enough not to open her door to men like Scoville? A babe in the woods.

"He said he really was sorry for what happened," Hannah persisted defensively. Jarrett narrowed his eyes and said nothing. After a moment her nerve broke, just as he had known it would. "And to tell me his wife was divorcing him," she concluded in a low mumble.

Jarrett closed his eyes in disgust and swore with soft violence. "To tell you his wife was leaving him. Let me see if I can finish this, shall I? He was very upset and wondered if you'd let him stay here for the night, right? It was really you he'd wanted all along. He'd only been staying with his wife for the kids' sake, and now that she had taken the initiative and filed for divorce he was free to come to you at last."

Hannah was staring at him in bewilderment. "How did you know about the kids?" she asked, tacitly agreeing to the rest.

Jarrett stifled another rough oath and surged to his feet. "A wild shot in the dark," he told her derisively. "Oh, hell, Hannah. That tale's as old as the hills. Don't tell me you were on the verge of buying it. You can't want a man like that!"

"I never said I wanted him!"

Restlessly Jarrett got to his feet and began pacing the room. He mustn't lose his control. That would really frighten her. He must remember to keep everything calm and deliberate. Gentle. Tender. Sensitive. It was time to exercise all those fine qualities he'd never had occasion to use before. But lack of use had a penalty that was becoming obvious.

He wasn't proving to be very good in the role of gentle, tender, sensitive, understanding protector. Dammit, he'd keep trying.

"Hannah, you need me. You'll come home with me tomorrow. We can take the pets with us and see about having the rest of your things moved at a later date," he began carefully.

"Damn you, Jarrett Blade, what makes you think I have any intention at all of letting you take over my life like this?" Hannah gulped another sip of the whiskey and watched him as he stalked back and forth in front of her.

He ran his hand through his hair, fighting for control. "It's obvious that you need me to look after you. I'll treat you well, Hannah. I'll keep you safe from all the people in the world who use women like you, and I'll give you everything you need and most of what you want."

"Does that mean you'll decide which of the things I want are really good for me?" she drawled from behind him.

If she didn't cut out the sarcasm, Jarrett decided resolutely, he really couldn't be responsible for his actions. "Hannah, you're going to have to trust me."

"Why?" she asked simply, taking another long swallow of the whiskey. Maybe he shouldn't have poured her quite so much, Jarrett thought with a frown.

"Because I say so!" At once he realized how irrational that sounded. "Look, honey, stop trying to bait me and just let me explain how it's going to be between the two of us."

"Ah, yes. The famous bargain you tried to make in Hawaii." She nodded wisely. "I'm supposed to love, honor, and obey, and in return I get security and a brick wall built around me to keep out the rest of the world. Big deal. I'm not interested, Jarrett. Try your fine bargain on some other unsuspecting female. I'm not that naive or that soft in the head, in spite of what you think. I don't need you or your great bargain." She took another swallow of the whiskey.

Jarrett felt his control slipping. This wasn't going at all the way he'd planned it. Tossing back the remainder of his own drink, Jarrett set the glass down on the nearest end table with due care. He was fully aware that he wasn't functioning with his usual controlled precision.

"Hannah, whether you realize it or not, you do need me." He called on reason. "Look at the mess you'd have been in with the Clydemores if I hadn't come along."

"No mess at all, as far as I can see," she said flippantly. "Alice Clydemore would have collected her stray 'souvenir' and we would have gone our separate ways."

"Doesn't it bother you that they used you?" Jarrett asked furiously.

"They aren't that much different from you, are they, Jarrett?"

It was too much. Jarrett forgot all his good intentions and decided to revert to Plan B. *Take the woman to bed and make love to her until she can't do anything except surrender,* he heard a small, primitive voice in his head advise. With a groan he paced forward, yanked Hannah's half-empty glass out of her hand, and pulled her to her feet.

"I'm not using you," he ground out. "You need me, Hannah Prescott."

"I don't need you or anyone else!"

"You're lying. And I'm going to prove you're lying," he vowed. He brought his mouth close to hers, and his eyes locked with her stormy ones. "We'll start with the most basic area in which you need me and we'll work up from here. I'm going to take you to bed, Hannah Prescott, and show you just how much you need me there. Then we'll see if you can't be a little more reasonable."

"Reasonable!" she gasped. "*Reasonable!* You call that reasonable? I won't—"

He cut off her next words by crushing her mouth beneath his own. The tremor that went through her body seemed to flood him with desire. It also flooded him with triumph and relief, because he knew instinctively it was a tremor of more than just anger.

"Hannah," he muttered against her mouth. "Honey, you want this as much as I do. How can you deny it?" Instead of giving her a chance to answer, he filled her mouth with his tongue. The soft moan that came from deep in her throat was all the answer he needed, Jarrett told himself. God, she was soft. And when her fingertips found their trembling way to his shoulders he remembered that there was more than an inviting softness in Hannah. There was a deep passion in her, too.

He wanted to be the only one to set that passion free.

"That's it, sweetheart, let me feel your need. Don't be afraid of it or of me, Hannah. Just give yourself to me. I'll make it good for you." He only half heard the low rumble of the reassuring words which he ground out against her mouth and throat. He only knew he meant them.

"Jarrett, please, no. Don't do this to me. I don't want this…"

Jarrett stifled the plea by kissing her again. With a rough groan of desire he slid his hands down her body, shaping the delightful curves of breast and thigh.

"You were made for me, honey," he breathed as he cupped the rounded contour of her buttocks and pulled her intimately close. "You need me and you want me. Why are you fighting me?"

"Jarrett, you don't understand. It's not enough!" Hannah whispered. But the words were spoken on a note of surrender as her head sank down on his shoulder.

"I'll make it enough. I'll make it everything you need," he vowed. Jarrett moved, sweeping her up into his arms. By God, he would make it perfect. He'd show her she didn't need anything or anyone else except him. With Hannah in his arms he glanced around impatiently and spotted the hall that must lead to the bedroom.

He felt a little light-headed, but he also felt incredibly strong. Hannah was a satisfying weight as he carried her down the carpeted hall to a room that was filled with plants. The bed in the center looked as if it were in the middle of a jungle bower. Huge ferns cascaded over the headboard and tall palms swayed around the flower-printed comforter. Ruffles and flounces had been used everywhere. Underneath the jungle setting was a deep, emerald-green carpet.

Jarrett grinned with a savage pleasure as he surveyed the very feminine, yet surprisingly primitive, room. "A man could disappear into a room like this and never emerge again. The goddess would look right at home here."

"The goddess..." Hannah broke off dazedly, lifting her head from his shoulder with an uncertain frown as if she were trying to make sense of a situation that had gone beyond her control. "Jarrett, we have to talk."

Jarrett hushed her gently, setting her down on the fluffy, flowered comforter. "We'll talk later." He sat down beside her, curving an arm around her thighs to make certain she didn't try to escape. With his other hand he reached down to deliberately begin undoing the buttons of the shirt she wore. At the first touch of his fingers on the bare skin of her throat Hannah went very still. Her eyes wide with apprehension and desire, she stared up at him.

"Why did you come here tonight?" she said thickly.

Jarrett shook his head once, unable to comprehend the question. Didn't she understand that she belonged to him now? Hadn't she guessed that he would follow her? "Why did you run from me?" he countered, sliding his fingers from one button to the next. "You knew I'd come after you."

"No." She shook her head, eyes closing briefly and then opening very wide once again. "No, I didn't know you'd

follow me. It makes no sense. You got what you wanted.
You got the goddess."

"And every time I look at her I think of you," he confided huskily. "She's pure female, just like you." His fingertips trailed lightly between the gentle hills of her breasts,
and he felt her responsive shiver. It echoed through his
own body, hardening it and sending a wave of reckless
wonder along his nerve endings.

Hannah wanted him; he could feel the desire in her. It
gave him a heady sense of masculine power to be able to
make this one particular woman respond, even against her
will. Jarrett realized vaguely that he'd never taken such
pleasure in a woman's response. But with Hannah it fed
something deep and primitive in him. Tonight he would
make her acknowledge the desire she felt and the underlying need.

"Tell me about it, honey," he growled as he pulled her
shirt free of the snug jeans.

"A-about what, Jarrett?" she asked shakily.

His mouth tilted slightly at the corners and he slowly
spread the opening of her shirt until he could see the crest
of one rose-tipped breast. Jarrett bent his head and nipped
the tightening bud with exquisite care. "Tell me what
you're feeling. Tell me about the heat that's building in
you. Tell me you need me, Hannah."

"You seem to have everything figured out for yourself," she managed with faint defiance, although she
gasped as he let her feel the edge of his teeth on the other
nipple.

"But you don't, apparently. I want you to figure it out
too, sweetheart. Tell me what it means; what it feels like
when your breasts harden like this. Tell me what those little shivers mean. Don't fight it, Hannah. Just give in to it.
Surrender. You're safe with me." Jarrett kept talking softly
as he found the fastening of her jeans. Hannah stiffened

again as he unsnapped them, her hand coming down pro-
testingly on top of his. "No, sweetheart. You don't want
me to stop. And it would be beyond my ability now, anyway. I'm aching for you, honey. I don't think I'll ever be
able to get enough of you. Something about you makes me
want you more than I've ever wanted any other woman in
my life. I want to take you until you can't do anything except respond. And I'm going to do just that. Now talk to
me, Hannah. Tell me what I want to hear."

"Jarrett, please!"

His own fingers were shaking a little now as he pushed
the tight-fitting jeans down over her hips. The scrap of lacy
panties came with them, revealing the dark, curling trian-
gle at the juncture of her legs. The promise of her complete nudity destroyed some of his methodical intent.
Jarrett let his fingers brush through the alluring tufts that
shielded the heart of her femininity. He felt, rather than
heard, the small moan that shook her.

"Can you tell me yet? Let me hear you say the words,
honey." Gently he encouraged her as he pushed the jeans
and the panties completely off her legs. Slowly he let his
palm glide back up her calf to the sensitive inner part of
her thigh. Dammit, he would make her tell him. She was
trembling with the force of her desire, and sooner or later
she would have to admit it aloud.

"Oh, Jarrett!"

She twisted on the comforter, her fingers clenching into
the fabric. Her eyes were closed now, and Jarrett could see
the way her mouth glistened as she dipped her tongue
along her lower lip. That small evidence of her heighten-
ing need was almost too much for his self-control. Grimly
he forced himself to slow down.

But his body was threatening to betray his willpower,
Jarrett acknowledged ruefully. His slacks were suddenly
far too confining and he wanted to feel her fingertips

prowling through the hair on his chest. With one hand stroking her warm body, Jarrett began stripping off his own shirt. Then he stood up briefly beside the bed to unfasten his slacks. A moment later he was naked, and he looked down to find Hannah watching him with feverish eyes. Part of the fever was desire and part of it was apprehension.

"Don't be afraid of me, honey," he murmured as he came down beside her and gathered her close. "Don't be afraid of needing me." Deliberately he stroked the length of her back down to her hip. Then he bent his head to kiss her with slow passion. When he felt the involuntary arching of her lower body he had to fight down an overwhelming rush of desire.

His head was beginning to spin. He couldn't think coherently any longer and he wasn't sure exactly what he was saying. He only knew he kept up a low, reassuring, encouraging pattern of words meant to draw Hannah more tightly into the web he was weaving.

"That's it, honey. Yes...touch me. Touch me, darling." Impatient with the uncertain exploration of his body, Jarrett took her hand and forced it gently lower. When her fingers at last cupped his manhood, he groaned. Then he began to stroke the pulsing bud between her legs until she cried out and clung to him.

"Jarrett, Jarrett, please. Take me now. Make love to me, Jarrett."

"Do you need me, Hannah?" God, if she didn't admit her need of him soon he would not be able to hold back. His body was throbbing with demand, his senses clamoring for the final coupling.

"Yes, Jarrett. Yes, I need you." The words were a sigh against his shoulder.

"Ah, sweetheart, that's all I wanted to hear. Hold on to me. Hold on tight."

The heat in his own body was a flame now, and it could only be extinguished in the liquid warmth of Hannah. Urgently Jarrett pushed her deep into the softness of the comforter. Then he lowered himself onto the greater softness of her body.

Her legs parted for him, and he knew a sense of burning triumph and pleasure as she openly demonstrated her need. "So soft. So soft and hot and melting..." He widened the space between her legs with his hands. "Put your legs around me, sweetheart," he groaned, and when she did so he let himself sink down along the length of her until he was pushing at the core of her.

"Jarrett, oh my God, Jarrett..."

He surged slowly into her, overcoming the tight tension that seemed to grip her at the last moment, just as it had the first time. She was so tight and warm and sexy. And he loved the feel of her legs wrapped around his hips. She was perfect, and he told her so as he began to move slowly within her.

"So sweet, so loving... Honey, you're all I want. Perfect."

Her arms went around his neck and she clung to him with shivering need, accepting the pace he set for their sensual journey. Through timeless moments of spiraling wonder and passion he guided her, glorying in the way she responded beneath him. She was his. His to arouse and satisfy. His to tantalize and release. His to care for and protect.

And she needed him. Tonight she had admitted it in one way. The rest would follow. That knowledge sent another rush of hot pleasure through his veins, and Jarrett knew he could not last much longer. The woman had a dazzling effect on his senses. But he had to make certain she was satisfied first. It was his duty and his pleasure as her lover. And the thrill of satisfying her was overpowering.

Inserting his fingers between their bodies, he found her exquisitely sensitive bud of desire. He touched her with care, and she responded explosively.

"Hannah, sweet Hannah," he breathed as she convulsed delightfully beneath him. He drove deeply into her. A tiny, choked cry was accompanied by the feel of her little teeth on his shoulder. The small pain sent him over the edge. His own cry of completion was a near shout of satisfaction and he buried the sound in the curve of her throat.

A long time later Jarrett stirred lazily to look down into the face of the woman he had just claimed and realized she had fallen asleep. He smiled to himself, arranging her carefully in the curve of his arm. Everything was going to be fine now. She would move in with him this week, and soon he would know what it was like to be the focus of her warmth and love.

Hannah needed him.

Seven

Hannah awoke the next morning with an overwhelming sensation of having just met her fate.

Blinking uncertainly in the morning light that cascaded into the room, she struggled upright in bed and gazed, appalled, at the sleeping man beside her. Jarrett sprawled in her bed as if he owned it, his magnificently nude body a dark, masculine counterpoint to the leafy, feminine setting. His somber brown hair was tousled and the lines of his face seemed less severe.

Urgently Hannah shoved aside the comforter. He must have pulled it over both of them sometime during the night. Good Lord! Had she gone crazy? What in the world had she been thinking of to let herself be so thoroughly seduced again by this man?

But when she had opened the door to him it had been as though her original fantasy had once more sprung to life. Only this time the fantasy had been augmented by real life memories of passion and desire and love.

For when she had seen him standing in her doorway last night, Hannah had known that what she felt for Jarrett Blade was love. Inexplicable, ungovernable, overwhelming love.

The restlessness she had been feeling since her return home, the lingering memories, the aching longing were all put to rest when she opened the door.

But nothing had changed, she told herself wildly as she let Erasmus outside for his morning run and checked on Siegfried, whose cage she had neglected to cover the previous evening. Nothing had changed. Jarrett still thought in terms of control and desire. He wanted her, but he didn't have the vaguest idea of how to love her.

"What a mess!" Hannah sighed at her reflection in the bathroom mirror. "Why did it have to be this man?"

She felt trapped and cornered, caught in a dilemma for which there didn't appear to be any easy answers. It wasn't fair that the one man capable of turning her ordered, serene existence upside down was altogether wrong for her. Jarrett Blade had a shadowy past and a rather foggy present, and he knew nothing about love except that he thought it might be nice to have her love him.

"I don't understand it, Siegfried," she announced to the parakeet as she began making breakfast with a vengeance. The bird sat contentedly in his cage, responding to her conversation with a running patter of bird talk that consisted of his normal chirps interspersed with the human vocabulary he had picked up. "I just don't understand the mess or the man. What am I going to do? I'm not sure I can get rid of him and I'm not sure I want to anyway."

After cracking the shells with an almost violent snap, Hannah briskly beat the scrambled eggs. Her brows drew together in a dark frown as she yanked whole grain bread

out of its plastic wrapper and shoved it rather brutally into
the toaster.

"Handsome Siegfried. Handsome Siegfried," the bird
announced, surveying his preened image in the cage
mirror.

"I know you're handsome, Siegfried. That doesn't solve
my problem."

"Love you. Love you. Love you."

"That's just it. He doesn't love me. He...he seems to
want me, but he doesn't love me. He wants me to love him,
Siegfried. A one-way street."

"Fantasy man. Fantasy man. Fantasy man."

"Where the hell did you learn that?" Hannah complained. Then she realized he must have picked it up from
her since she had returned from Hawaii. "Look, do me a
favor and don't say that in front of him, okay?"

"What shouldn't you say in front of me, Siegfried?"
Jarrett's deep, lazy drawl brought Hannah's head up with
a snap, and she turned to see him standing in the doorway
of her sunny kitchen. His hair was intriguingly damp from
the shower and his shirt was open a couple of buttons, revealing the beginnings of the crisp mat of hair she remembered so well. Below the khaki slacks he wore, his feet were
bare, making him look far too comfortably at home in her
kitchen.

"Never mind, he's just chattering," Hannah interrupted hastily, aware that her senses had leaped in response at the mere sight of him. What had this man done
to her?

Jarrett nodded at Siegfried and then came over to the
stove to drop a familiar, possessive little kiss on the nape
of Hannah's neck. "Smells good. I had a feeling you'd be
a good cook. Where's Erasmus?"

"He's still running around outside," Hannah mumbled, bending industriously over the eggs. What now?

Should she bring up the subject of last night? Should she initiate a confrontation? Order him out of her house? Oh, Lord. She didn't know what to do. She only knew that a part of her fiercely resisted the idea of sending Jarrett away. "There's coffee on the counter over there," she heard herself say.

"Great. I could use some." Jarrett poured himself a full mug from the automatic brewing pot and began to sip it, leaning back against the counter. He watched her as she deftly stirred the eggs into the pan. "How soon can you be ready to go?"

"Go? Go where?" She floundered a bit and almost dropped the spatula she was using to stir the eggs. Steadfastly she kept her eyes focused on the frying pan, ignoring the burning heat of his gaze.

"Home," he said gently.

"I am home."

"To my home, Hannah. Honey, don't be deliberately obtuse," he added softly.

She lifted her head to glare at him. "Maybe you're the one who's being obtuse, Jarrett. Do you realize I don't even know where you live?"

He blinked like a great cat and then grinned. "That's right, you don't, do you. Things got a little hectic in Hawaii and we never had time to talk properly. I live in northern California. Along the coast. A little town just south of the Oregon border. You'll like it."

Hannah drew a deep breath, unnerved by the satisfied self-assurance of the man. "Jarrett, I want to make something very clear..."

The sound of the doorbell interrupted her brave words. Frowning, she went to answer it and found Charlotte Pomeroy on the front step. She was surrounded by her three kids.

"Hi, Hannah. Sorry to bother you so early in the morning. I'm on my way to drop the kids off at day care and school, and I wanted to stop by and see if you'd gone ahead and reapplied for your old job. I talked to Edith down in Personnel yesterday and she said— Oh! I didn't realize you had company."

"Where's Erasmus?" the oldest of the Pomeroy children demanded, looking around for the dog, who was already bounding into the front yard to greet the new arrivals. "Come on, 'Rasmus. Let's go!" Scott and Corrie raced off with the dog. Jimmy, the youngest, looked up pleadingly.

"Can I see Siegfried?"

Charlotte hushed him. "Darling, you know you're not allowed to touch Siegfried."

"Just wanna see him!" Jimmy protested righteously.

"Come on in, Jimmy. Siegfried's in his cage. Charlotte, will you have some coffee? This is Jarrett Blade."

"How do you do, Mr. Blade," Charlotte murmured, obviously fascinated by the sight of the tall man standing just behind Hannah in the doorway. "Where did you come from? I had no idea Hannah was seeing anyone special these days..." She let the sentence trail off questioningly as she darted a slanting glance at Hannah.

"Call me Jarrett. Hannah and I met in Hawaii." As if he had been entertaining other people in Hannah's kitchen for years, he poured Charlotte a cup of coffee and sat down at the table with her. "Hannah, I think the eggs are burning."

"Oh, Lord! The eggs!" Flustered, Hannah quickly began to dish out breakfast, one eye on little Jimmy as he stood staring at Siegfried.

"Go right ahead and eat, you two. I won't stay long, I promise." Charlotte grinned. "I'm Charlotte Pomeroy, Jarrett. I used to work with Hannah."

"Really? I seem to be meeting a lot of Hannah's former co-workers lately."

"Who else have you met?" Charlotte demanded, surprised.

Hannah carried the plates over to the table. "Scoville came by last night," she muttered. "Jarrett arrived just after he did."

"Oh, my. That must have been interesting," Charlotte drawled.

"It was rather awkward, actually," Hannah began. She was interrupted by Jarrett.

"I think Scoville and I came to an understanding. He won't be bothering Hannah again." Calmly Jarrett attacked his eggs.

"I'd love to have seen the confrontation." Charlotte giggled. "Did Hannah tell you all about him? How he caused her to lose her job?"

"Yes. She won't have to worry about him again."

Charlotte nodded. "Because he was forced to resign himself."

"I wouldn't know about that." Jarrett shrugged, reaching for a slice of toast. "The reason Hannah won't have to worry about him is that she's coming to live with me in California."

"Hannah! Are you really?" Charlotte was suddenly all wide-eyed attention.

"Now just a minute," Hannah started and then her attention was caught by little Jimmy, who was attempting to crawl up on a plant stand to get closer to Siegfried. "Jimmy, get down from there," she admonished severely.

"Just wanna get closer," Jimmy complained, reluctantly climbing back down.

"Go 'way, kid. Go 'way, kid. Go 'way, kid." Siegfried glared down at the boy. Jimmy retreated with a sigh.

"When are you moving, Hannah?" Charlotte demanded.

It was Jarrett who answered; Hannah was too busy trying to marshal her confused responses. "I think we'll fly down today or tomorrow, depending on how long it takes Hannah to get ready. Of course, with all these pets it might be better to rent a car and drive," he said musingly.

"And don't forget the plants," Charlotte said with a wicked grin. "You can't separate Hannah from either her pets or her plants. I'm so glad she's finally settling down with a nice man. You have no idea how I'd worried about her living here with this zoo and no real family. She needs a real home with a man and some babies, don't you think? She's very good with kids. Loves 'em."

"Charlotte!" Hannah's protest was little more than a squeak of outrage. It went unnoticed.

Jarrett was alrady nodding complacently as he rose to help himself to more coffee. "My sentiments exactly. Hannah's a born mother. I'm going to give her precisely what she needs. I'm going to let her create a home for both of us. A real home."

"Oh, Hannah, this is so exciting! Jimmy, you heard Aunt Hannah. Get down from that plant stand before it topples over. Siegfried doesn't like you to get too close. Now, Hannah, what can I do to help? You'll need someone on this end taking care of the plants you have to leave behind. You can't possibly get them all in a car. Will you be selling the furniture? I'd love to have that little inlaid plant stand Jimmy's trying to demolish."

"Look, Charlotte, you don't understand. I'm not planning on going anywhere!"

"But Jarrett just said..."

"Don't pay any attention to him!" Hannah rasped, rising to her feet to confront the two adults in her kitchen.

A sudden pounding on the kitchen door announced the arrival of Erasmus and the other two children. All three bounded happily into the kitchen when Jarrett promptly opened the door.

"Hannah and I have a few things still to discuss," Jarrett explained easily as the kids and dog sailed past him, heading for the living room. He seemed pleasantly oblivious to the growing chaos around him.

"So I see. Well, let me tell you I'm solidly on your side," Charlotte announced. "Hannah needs someone like you."

"Yes, I know." Jarrett smiled, his gunmetal eyes on Hannah's harried expression. "She needs someone to take care of her."

Charlotte laughed as Hannah sputtered. "It's not that Hannah can't defend herself physically, of course. I mean, did she ever tell you exactly what happened between her and Doug Scoville?"

Jarrett's eyes narrowed fractionally. "I know he tried to get her into bed."

"He pestered her constantly until one night he actually followed her home and more or less assaulted her. The man simply couldn't believe she wasn't madly attracted to him. Hannah took care of him easily enough with her judo, but then his wife arrived on the scene and..."

"Her judo!" Jarrett interrupted in confusion. "What judo?"

"She's quite good at it," Charlotte explained in surprise. "Flattened poor Scoville right there on the living room rug. Corrie, you and Scott put down that turtle."

"I didn't know she knew judo," Jarrett said distantly, studying Hannah.

"I'd love to have seen the event. Unfortunately, it was Scoville's wife who saw it. She chose to put all the blame on Hannah. Accused Hannah of trying to seduce Scoville. Ridiculous. At any rate, she created such a fuss that

Scoville asked for Hannah's resignation. Rather than work under impossible circumstances, Hannah resigned. But now she's practically got her old job in the bag. Scoville's out of the picture and Personnel wants to rehire Hannah. Corrie, I said put down that turtle!''

"Please put Herbie back," Hannah said weakly, turning to see the two children hovering over the turtle's bowl. The whole place was in chaos. She couldn't seem to think straight. Jarrett was watching her with a curious expression in his eyes. Charlotte was chattering happily about Hannah's going off to California and the three children were scurrying around noisily. Erasmus was trotting happily around the table looking for handouts and Siegfried had set up a chattering counterpoint to all the commotion around him.

"Hannah has a chance at her old job?" Jarrett asked quietly.

"Oh, yes. She'll have no trouble at all getting it back if she wants it. But I guess she won't need it now, will she?"

"No," Jarrett stated with abrupt decision. "She won't need it. She needs other things now."

"Well, I'd better get these little turkeys out of here before they do any lasting damage," Charlotte said cheerfully, finishing her coffee and quickly getting to her feet. "Come on, kids. Back in the car."

"Ah, do we have to go? Can't we stay and play here?"

"Hannah is very busy today," Charlotte informed them severely. "In the car! Hannah, I'll call you later, all right? We can talk better on the phone. Jarrett, it was lovely to meet you. Take care and drive carefully. It's going to be a long trip with all those animals and plants in the car! I don't envy you."

Like a small whirlwind, Charlotte left the cozy little house with her family in tow. Hannah and Jarrett sat facing each other across the kitchen table as the sound of the car disappeared down the street. Slowly quiet and order returned to everything except Hannah's heart. She looked into Jarrett's unreadable eyes and desperately strove to take control of the situation.

"Jarrett, we have got to talk. This idiotic mess has gone far enough."

"You didn't tell me you knew judo. You didn't tell me you'd flattened Scoville."

"What's that got to do with anything?"

He looked as if he were going to say something and then changed his mind. "Nothing. It changes nothing. Hannah, you're coming to California with me."

"Dammit, will you listen to me? You can't just order me around like this, Jarrett! Don't you understand? I have a life of my own, and I'm not at all sure I want to abandon it for a...a..." The words failed her, but Siegfried happily supplied them.

"Fantasy man. Fantasy man. Fantasy man."

"I'm not a fantasy, Hannah," Jarrett said calmly. "Last night was no fantasy. I can make you want me again and again." He leaned forward intently. "You need me, honey. Last night in bed you admitted it."

"That's just sex!"

"It's a start!"

"It's not enough!"

"You love me. Admit it!" he ordered roughly.

"I'm not admitting anything!" she blazed.

"You did last night."

"Dammit, Jarrett, I will not allow you to railroad me into an arrangement based purely on sex!"

"It's not based purely on sex. There's a hell of a lot more involved than that," he bit out savagely.

"Is that so? Then prove it!" she challenged recklessly without pausing to think.

"How?" he countered at once, startling her. His eyes were almost silver as he regarded her across the short distance of the table.

She ought to slow down and think about what she was saying, Hannah realized. But there was no stopping the impulsive words that sprang to her lips. She had been driven too far. "If you're not just interested in a short affair based strictly on sex, then let's hear you invite me down to California for an affair without any sex!"

"What?" Jarrett surged to his feet, filling her kitchen with menace and sudden, vast, masculine annoyance. "What the devil are you talking about?"

"You heard me," she managed bravely. "If you're offering something more than a sexual affair, you can damn well prove it. Do you want friendship? Companionship? A home? What do you want, Jarrett? If it's not just sex you're after, tell me what it is you do want."

"Dammit, I'm not looking for a platonic affair!" he raged, gripping the back of the chair in which he had been sitting. "And neither are you! You like what we have together in bed, whether or not you'll admit it! You don't want to give it up any more than I do!"

"I can give it up. Can you? Or is that really all you want from me?"

"You little witch! Do you honestly think I'd chase all over the Northwest after you just for the sake of a roll in the sack?" he shot back brutally.

"I don't know," she cried. "I honestly don't know what you'd do for sex. Because I don't know you very well at all, do I, Jarrett Blade? That's my whole point, damn you! I don't know you! Yet you're asking me to give up everything to come and have an affair with you. Who the hell do you think you are?"

"I'm the man who's going to take care of you!" he gritted.

"But I don't need you to take care of me! I've got a good job waiting for me. I can handle men like Scoville with my judo. I have enough common sense not to let people use me, in spite of what you think. I've been existing very nicely for twenty-nine years and I can go on just as pleasantly. No matter how good you are in bed, you're not going to lure me to California with sex!"

"You're not making any sense!" he raged. "You're saying you'll come to California for a non-sexual affair even though you like what we have in bed. But when I offer you sex, you say you won't come with me? You're crazy, woman!"

"Which only goes to show how little you know about me!"

He shot her a furious glance as he strode to the kitchen doorway. "I know a hell of a lot more about you than you seem to realize, little hellcat." He paused in the doorway, confronting her with the full impact of his intimidating presence. "I know you're going to regret this little scene the minute I walk out that door. When I'm back in California and you're up here alone except for this zoo, you're going to think a lot about what you've thrown away. You're a passionate woman, Hannah Prescott. I don't think you realized just *how* passionate until you met me, did you?"

"Jarrett!"

"You're behaving like an emotional little fool, and I'm going to teach you a lesson. I'm going back to California this morning and I'm going to let you simmer for a while. I'm going to let you think about it for a time and then I'll call you up and see if you've changed your mind. I'm betting you will change your mind, Hannah. I'm betting I know you a whole lot better than you know yourself."

"Jarrett, wait!"

He was already in the bedroom, pulling on his shoes. She arrived at the door in time to see him finish tying the laces. "Wait for what, Hannah? More of your crazy ideas?"

"Jarrett, if you would just listen to me..."

"I have been listening. And all I've been hearing is nonsense." He straightened and came toward her. She backed nervously down the hall in front of him. He reached into his hip pocket for the car keys. "An affair without any sex. Talk about nonsense! You can't hold out five minutes when I decide to seduce you. Admit that much, at least, Hannah. Don't be a complete hypocrite!"

"I...I know I can't," she whispered sadly as he backed her down the hall and into the living room. "That's why you'd have to give me your word you wouldn't attempt to seduce me. You'd have to promise to keep your end of the bargain. Jarrett... Oh!"

The exclamation came out as he suddenly walked her right back against the wall and caged her with his arms. Hannah swallowed nervously as she found herself looking up into Jarrett's glowering face.

"Going to try your judo on me?" he challenged coolly. "I'll warn you right now that I've had a lot of karate training. Shall we see who can flatten whom?"

"Jarrett, please, you're being unreasonable," she got out through dry lips.

"I'm being unreasonable?" he echoed in astonishment. "I'm behaving with an amazing amount of restraint under the circumstances! I ought to turn you over my knee and then take you to bed. But I think you need a more effective lesson than that. You need a little time to realize what you're throwing away."

"I'm only asking for a little time to find out if we really have something meaningful together," Hannah pleaded, knowing that the whole situation was disintegrating and there was nothing she could do about it. Tears already threatened to close her throat, but she would not give in to them. Not yet. There would be plenty of time after Jarrett Blade had left.

"I'll give you that time," he snarled. "You can spend it alone, though. I think you'll be able to come to a much quicker conclusion that way." He straightened suddenly and stalked to the door, flinging it open. "If you change your mind before I get around to calling you, here's my number." He yanked his thin wallet out of his pocket and extracted a small white card. He tossed it down on the nearest plant stand.

Before Hannah could peel herself away from the wall, he was gone, the door slammed shut behind him. Erasmus stood at attention, ears cocked, listening as Jarrett drove off. Herbie poked his head out of his shell, where he had taken refuge.

But it was Siegfried who made the most intelligent statement concerning the situation.

"Fantasy man. Fantasy man. Fantasy man," he chanted in a subdued tone.

Eight

Dammit, she didn't need him. Not the way he had thought. He had been so certain...

Bitterly Jarrett returned the rental car at the airport and started the trek from one airline counter to the next, trying to find a flight back to California. It didn't take long. He was soon on his way. But as he settled back into the seat, waving aside the scrambled eggs being offered on the breakfast flight, he began to question his usually sound judgment.

How had he mismanaged things so badly? It wasn't like him. He generally had everything neatly under control in his life. But he'd never dealt with a woman like Hannah Prescott. Dammit! He'd been so determined to handle her correctly this time around. No more mistakes.

But he'd sure made a huge error assuming that she needed him. The truth was that she really seemed to get along fine on her own. Judo. His mouth curved downward in dismay. Who would have guessed that a soft little woman like Hannah knew enough judo to throw Scoville on his back? And it sounded as if she had her old job back if she wanted it. Her home was cozy and comfortable. It didn't seem to need a man in it at all.

The only place he seemed to fit was in her bed, and she didn't even want that! A platonic affair, she said! Of all the stupid, idiotic, pointless exercises in frustration!

Jarrett accepted coffee from the hostess and studied the seat-back in front of him. An affair without any sex. Why the hell would she want that? Sex seemed to be about all she needed from him. It didn't make any sense.

Face it, Blade, he gritted silently, it's not that you couldn't make yourself abide by her terms for a while, although it would be tough. It's that you're afraid to abide by them.

Now he was getting to the truth of the matter, he realized with disgust. He was afraid to grant Hannah's crazy request because he would be denying himself the one hold he did have on her.

Why was it so important that he maintain that claim?

Maybe *he* was the one who needed *her*.

That thought sent a cold chill down his back. Grimly Jarrett requested another cup of hot coffee. If it wasn't for the fact that it was only nine-thirty in the morning, he'd have asked for something a lot stronger.

It took more willpower than Hannah could possibly have guessed to pull herself back together after the scene the morning Jarrett left. It was harder this time than it had been when she had left him in Hawaii—harder because she had acknowledged her love for him.

For an entire week following his abrupt departure she made herself go through the motions of day-to-day routine. She saw her friends, watered her plants, chatted with her animals. And she tried her damnedest not to give in to the tears or the pain.

What good was a relationship with the man of her dreams if it wasn't founded on something far more solid than a sexual liaison? Over and over again she asked herself that question, and always she seemed to be left hanging without a reassuring answer.

Charlotte phoned toward the end of the week, not for the first time, demanding to know why she was still in town.

"You're crazy not to go to him, you know that, don't you? You're not going to get a better offer, my girl. Take him up on it!" her friend urged.

"Thanks! I'm really not doing all that badly on my own, you know," Hannah retorted caustically.

"Hah! Just remember what I said about starting your family soon. Harry and I already had Corrie and Scott by the time I was your age."

"Charlotte, I don't want to discuss this."

"I hear from Personnel that they've made you an offer. Going to take it instead of heading for California?"

"Probably. They increased my salary considerably. I'd be a fool not to take it." Hannah sighed.

"I would have said the same thing last week. But now I know you've got a better offer."

"An affair? With a man I hardly know? A man who keeps insisting I need him and that I love him but who doesn't need or love me? That's a better offer?"

"Calm down. You're getting excited."

"You're damn right I'm getting excited! I'm about at my wit's end! The only man I've been really attracted to in years wants only an affair, and my best friend is encouraging me to go through with it!"

"Hannah, do you want to spend the rest of your life talking to a turtle and a parakeet and a dog?"

"Why not? At least I know where I stand with them. They need me!"

"And you don't think your fantasy man does?" Charlotte shot back.

"No, frankly, I don't. If he does, he isn't capable of admitting it. Besides, I want more than that, Charlotte. I want to be loved. Really loved," Hannah whispered morosely. "I want it all."

"Sometimes a woman has to take what she can get," Charlotte lectured cryptically.

"You're a fine one to talk. Three beautiful children, a good job, and a loving, supportive husband. Don't tell me I've got to take less than that."

"All right, Hannah. I'll back off. But promise me you'll think about it, okay? I liked Jarrett Blade. There was something about him that made me think he'd be good for you."

"You figured that out from meeting him one morning over breakfast?"

Hannah hung up the phone a few minutes later with a feeling of being greatly put upon. She looked at Erasmus, who was dozing at her feet. "I don't even know if his offer is still open," she whispered sadly. "He never called as he said he would, Erasmus."

She reached into Herbie's bowl and plucked him out just as the phone rang again. Hannah was still holding Herbie at eye level, about to tell him what a fine-looking turtle he was when she said hello rather absently into the receiver.

"Hannah?"

The sound of Jarrett's voice nearly made her drop Herbie. "Jarrett!" Carefully she set down Herbie, then she lowered herself rather shakily into the nearest chair. "Jarrett?"

This was it, Hannah thought. He was going to make his magnanimous offer again after letting her suffer for a week. Of all the arrogant nerve! Of all the chauvinistic, outrageous, masculine nerve! What in the world was she going to do?

"Hannah, I'm calling to see if you'll come to California," Jarrett said quietly, without any emotion at all that Hannah could detect. "I'll accept your terms."

It was a good thing she had put down Herbie, Hannah realized vaguely. She surely would have dropped him by this time. "My terms?" she managed weakly.

"We'll try it your way for a while." There was a lengthy pause during which Hannah tried to corral her racing thoughts. And then Jarrett asked coolly, "Hannah? Will you come?"

She answered before she could stop to think. "I'll come, Jarrett. I'll be there in a couple of days."

There was a beat of silence on the other end of the line. "I'll fly up and drive down with you," Jarrett finally announced gruffly.

"No, no that won't be necessary, Jarrett. I'd prefer to drive down by myself. It's only an overnight trip. I'll...I'll see you day after tomorrow."

God, they were discussing this as if it were a casual holiday trip. What on earth did she think she was doing? But it was done. Jarrett had actually told her to come on her own terms. Hannah said good-bye after another long pause during which neither of them seemed to be able to say anything intelligent. And then she threw herself back into the chair and regarded her pets.

"We're going to California, pals. Don't ask me why. I'm not sure myself. But we're going."

But the next morning, as she got behind the wheel of her little compact, Hannah knew exactly why she was going to California with Herbie and Erasmus and Siegfried and

Yolanda and Ludmilla. She was going because she was
letting herself dare to hope.

The hope was that Jarrett Blade had discovered he
needed her for some other reason than to warm his bed.

Somewhere after crossing the Oregon border it did oc-
cur to her to wonder whether or not he'd lied in order to
get her to California. But Hannah only took her foot off
the pedal for a few seconds at the thought.

"He wouldn't lie to me," she told her passengers. Erasmus, who was sitting in the front seat beside her, whimpered in agreement. There was an even more dangerous
possibility, Hannah admitted silently, and that was that she
might be lying to herself. Jarrett Blade seemed to be a law
unto himself. He appeared to make his own rules as he
went along, and if she deluded herself into thinking he was
capable of needing more from a woman than just sex, she
would have only herself to blame when she got hurt in the
end.

Even as the mountainous scenery of Interstate 5 through
Oregon unfolded outside the car's windows, however,
Hannah knew she no longer had a choice. She was
committed.

Hannah and her passengers spent the night near Med-
ford, Oregon, and the next morning they made their way
over to the coast and Highway 101. From there they wound
their way down the picturesque California coastline until
Hannah found the small town Jarrett had named on the
phone.

The place would have made a charming watercolor
scene, she mused as she guided the little car through the
center of town. It had been a major fishing village once,
and boats of all kinds still thronged the harbor. Some were
still working craft, but many were clearly pleasure boats.
Did Jarrett sail? Hannah sighed. Just one more thing she
didn't know about the man.

Through the weatherbeaten town and out along the cliffs on the far side, she carefully followed Jarrett's terse directions. The house, when she finally found it, was not quite what she'd expected. Or then again, perhaps it was. It did, after all, fit Jarrett very well.

Isolated, weathered, and strong-looking, it, too, would have made an interesting watercolor. It seemed rather large for a man who lived alone, Hannah thought as she brought the car to a halt in the curving drive and studied the place for a moment before climbing out. It was two stories high, and she wondered what he did with all the extra space. The only really inviting aspect was the huge porch that wrapped the old place. Now, in summer, it would be a very comfortable area to sit and watch the sea at sundown. Jarrett really ought to put a nice porch swing on that veranda, she said to herself. And a garden out back might be nice too....

Hannah threw open the car door and got out, reaching for Herbie's bowl as she did so. Erasmus bounded out behind her and instantly began exploring the new terrain. Hannah was opening the backseat door and reaching inside for Siegfried's cage when she heard Jarrett's voice.

"Hannah!"

She whirled, cage in one hand and Herbie in the other, and suddenly she felt horribly nervous. Jarrett stood on the porch, devouring the sight of her as if he couldn't quite understand what she was doing there. His hard face was carved in intent, harsh lines and the gunmetal eyes were shadowed and smoky. He was dressed in a pair of khaki slacks, as usual, and the sleeves on his khaki shirt were rolled up to reveal his sinewy arms. The breeze off the ocean caught and ruffled his hair as he stood, hands braced on the porch railing, and regarded her.

Hannah bit her lip and wondered what the hell she was doing there. Dressed in a casual white shirt and sandals, and jeans that hugged her rounded figure, she felt awkward and uncertain. Even the prim, coiled braids on her head didn't supply the regal arrogance she wanted to use in self-defense.

For a long moment they simply stared at each other. Only Erasmus seemed at ease. He skittered around Jarrett, barking loudly. The spell between the two humans was broken when Jarrett finally reached down to pat the dog on the head.

"Hello, Hannah. I was getting worried," Jarrett began slowly as he came down the steps.

What was he thinking? Hannah swallowed and then rushed into conversation in an effort to cover her nervousness. Clutching Herbie's bowl and Siegfried's cage, she started forward.

"Actually, I was getting a little worried myself. The only motel I could find last night had a huge 'No Pets' sign up, and I had to smuggle Erasmus and Herbie and Siegfried inside when no one was looking. Then this morning when I let Erasmus out for a few minutes a maid spotted us and I thought we were done for. I had visions of having to leave Oregon on the lam or, worse, having to phone you for bail bond money for these three. Fortunately we managed to escape. I think the maid had second thoughts about turning us all in. Where shall I put Herbie?"

She breezed into the house, aware that Jarrett was right behind her, and stopped short. Before she could speak, however, Jarrett said softly, "I wasn't worried so much that you might be in jail as I was that you'd changed your mind altogether about coming, Hannah," he said gently.

Hannah ignored the statement, surveying the room in which she found herself with startled horror. "Good grief! It looks like a museum!"

Glass cases seemed to line every wall. Countless pots, statues, carvings, masks, and textiles were displayed behind the glass. At the far end a wall full of intimidating tomes completed the scene. In between there was a formal grouping of dark, heavy furniture.

"You can put Herbie down on that end table," Jarrett said abruptly, taking the turtle's bowl from her hand. "And maybe Siegfried could go over there." He indicated the top of a glass case. "Hannah? Are you all right? What's the matter?"

"Nothing. Nothing at all. it's just that I don't see how you can live with all these museum pieces around you." Hannah shook herself and then obediently carried Siegfried over to the glass counter.

"Most of these things have never seen the inside of a museum," Jarrett growled, watching her with a frown. "This is a private collection. Very private."

"Oh." Hannah stared around her. It figured. Her fantasy man lived in a private museum filled with pre-Columbian artifacts. She must be crazy to think she could change a man who preferred the company of the dead past to the living present. For a few seconds she was almost overcome with doubt. Then Siegfried interrupted her grim thoughts.

"New home. New home. New home," he announced happily, bouncing back and forth along his perch.

Hannah grimaced and set him down over a carving of a leering god. "He, uh, picked that up from me on the trip down," she explained in a mumble.

Jarrett came forward suddenly, taking her shoulders in a firm grip and turning her to face him. "Hannah, is that how you think of this place? As a new home?"

"Well, uh, yes, I suppose I do." She wiped her damp palms on her jeans and lifted her chin proudly. "Of course, it's going to need a great deal of work to turn this old museum of yours into a home, but I'll see what can be done. In the meantime, which is my room?" She looked him directly in the eye as she asked that question.

Jarrett hesitated. "You've very sure this is the way you want it?"

"I'm sure."

"For how long, Hannah?"

"Until I change my mind," she retorted firmly. "Which room, Jarrett?"

He held her for a moment longer and then released her "Second door at the top of the stairs. I, uh, put some fresh sheets on the bed this morning."

Hannah blinked, touched. "Why, thank you. I'll just get my suitcases from the car..."

"I'll get them for you."

"Actually, if you really want to do me a favor"—she grinned suddenly—"you can bring in Ludmilla and Yolanda. I couldn't bear to leave them behind with the others. They're like family, you see. But they weigh a ton each, and I'd much rather carry the suitcases."

"I'll get the plants."

A polite, uncertain wariness hovered between Hannah and Jarrett for the rest of the day. Only the animals seemed quite content. Jarrett was treating her almost as a guest Hannah realized. He showed her around the rambling old house, took her for a walk on the beach, and stood watching from the doorway when she unpacked her suitcases.

Dinner was a studied, exquisitely polite affair. Hannah cooked it, directing Jarrett to make the salad and pour the wine. "This is good stuff," she approved, sampling the excellent California vintage she was drinking. "Do you have a wine cellar stashed somewhere among all this old junk?" The wine had helped remove some of her nervousness.

Jarrett paused in the act of forking his asparagus. " have a small cellar down in the basement."

"Well, that's something at least," Hannah mumbled.

"I don't exactly consider these things 'junk,'" he went on carefully.

"Yes, well, as we discovered in Hawaii, junk is in the eye of the beholder, isn't it?" Hannah retorted. She polished off the last of her wine and held out her glass for more. She had the feeling she was going to need it. The task that lay ahead of her was daunting in the extreme.

After dinner he gallantly showed her into the living room and poured her a glass of brandy. Then her gaze fell on the wall of books at the far end of the room. "Are all those books about pre-Columbian art?" she asked.

"Most of them, yes."

"How unfortunate. I didn't bring anything with me to read. I was rather hoping you might have a few racy thrillers lying around somewhere. Who would have guessed there were so many books about these old bits of pottery? Where did you get them all, Jarrett?"

His mouth curved wryly. "One or two of them I wrote," he said softly.

Hannah snapped her head around to stare at him as he sat down beside her on the sofa. "You wrote them? Good heavens. I think I'm impressed."

"Coming from you, that's a compliment." He sipped his brandy and watched her over the rim of the glass.

"Is that how you make a living? Writing books about all these artifacts?" She waved a hand at the contents of the glass cases. "I've just realized I have no clear idea of your work, Jarrett." Actually, she'd realized that much earlier, but she hadn't known quite how to bring up the subject.

"Among other things. I also do occasional appraisals."

"For whom?" She frowned.

"I act as a consultant for museums and, very rarely, Customs."

"No kidding? What else do you do? I mean, is ther
enough money in that to enable you to indulge your, uh
hobby?"

"Collecting pre-Columbian art is not exactly m
hobby," Jarrett said gently.

"No, it's your passion, isn't it?" she sighed. "Wel
what else do you do besides write books about it an
consult?"

"Occasionally I take on certain jobs," he said slowly.

"What sort of jobs?" she demanded.

"Jobs like the one that took me to Hawaii."

Hannah chewed on her lower lip. "I see. You help peo
ple recover lost or stolen pre-Columbian art?"

"Sometimes."

'And there's enough money in all that to keep you in ol
bits and pieces of junk?" She grinned.

"I get by," he drawled. "Of course, now that I have
few extra mouths to feed, I might have to do a bit mor
consulting. Or a little dealing. That's something else I do
I act as a broker for private collectors."

Hannah seized on the one point that mattered to he
"About these extra mouths…"

"You don't have to worry, honey. I told you I was not
poor man. I'm not outrageously wealthy by any mean
but I can take care of you and the zoo." Jarrett absentl
reached down to his feet to fondle Erasmus's ears. The do
stretched out blissfully.

"Jarrett," Hannah began determinedly, "I don't wa
you to think that we're all going to move in here an
mooch off you. As soon as we find out whether or no
this…this relationship of ours is going to work out, I'll g
a job."

"No." He sipped his brandy.

Hannah's brows came together in a firm line. "C
course I will. I've worked ever since I got out of college.

don't intend to stop now. Besides, as you pointed out, there are a lot of mouths to feed here. You shouldn't have to be responsible for the ton of dog food Erasmus eats!''

"I can afford you and Herbie and Erasmus and the bird. There's no need for you to work."

Hannah drew in her breath and let it out slowly. "Be reasonable, Jarrett. We don't have any idea how well our *association* is going to work out. Sooner or later you'll probably get tired of me or I'll knock over one of your precious pots and you'll strangle me. One way or another this relationship could be terminated abruptly. Frankly, I don't want to find myself stranded without a job. And it's difficult to get back into the work force once you've been out of it for a while. I'd rather keep working."

"We can discuss it later."

"What on earth is the problem? I knew you were domineering and chauvinistic, but somehow I didn't think you were going to be this primitive!" she stormed.

His mouth hardened. "Can't you just trust me? I can take care of you."

"You're missing the point! Women these days work. You can't have spent your entire life buried in a pre-Columbian grave!"

"We'll discuss it some other time," he told her tightly.

Hannah groaned and swallowed the remainder of her brandy. "This is hopeless, isn't it? I don't know what I'm doing here. I should be back in Seattle getting ready to restart my old job."

"It's too late for that, Hannah. You're here." Jarrett's dark voice was like a slab of granite. Inflexible, unmoving, as certain as time. "And now that you are here, how long do you intend to keep up this game you're making us play?"

Hannah stiffened. "It's not a game, Jarrett."

"Are you afraid of me?" he pressed more gently
"Afraid of what I can make you feel?" His eyes wer
suddenly warm now, smoky and molten. Hopeful?

"Of course not!"

"Then why deny us both what we want?" Jarrett pu
down his brandy glass and stroked her cheek with hi
finger.

"Jarrett, you promised..."

"I'm not going to make love to you. I only want t
know how long you're going to make me wait?" he mui
mured. "A day or two? A week?"

"I can't put a time limit on it!" she gasped.

"You expect me to wait indefinitely?"

"Jarrett, you agreed to this," she protested weakly
aware that if he decided to seduce her tonight she would b
helpless to resist. "I trusted you."

He dropped his hand and sank back into the corner o
the couch, some of the warmth leaving his eyes. "Is tha
how you plan to keep me in line? By reminding me tha
you had my word on this crazy arrangement?"

"If that's what it takes."

"Hannah, I won't wait forever. You do understan
that?"

"I don't see why not," she rallied bravely. "You're a
customed to dealing in terms of centuries. Just look at a
these old things. You're obviously quite capable of wai
ing for what you want. I'll bet you waited years before yo
acquired some of the choicer bits and pieces of th
collection."

"I won't wait years for you, honey. I'm not at all su
I'll even wait a few weeks. A few days is probably mo
likely. I won't let you keep me dangling."

"Then why in hell did you invite me to come down he
in the first place?" she blazed furiously. "I thought we ha

an agreement. We're supposed to be getting to know each other."

"Two weeks. At the end of two weeks we settle this issue."

"Says who?" she gritted.

"I say so," he countered mildly. "I want a woman, Hannah. Not a houseguest."

She narrowed her eyes and said nothing, but he must have sensed exactly what she was thinking.

"Going to run, Hannah? You tried that once before, remember? I'll find you again, just as I did last time."

"Threats, Jarrett?" she scoffed tiredly. "Is that the only way you know how to handle a woman? With threats?"

He blinked and frowned, and she was startled to realize that what she'd said had apparently made some kind of impact. He surged to his feet and stalked across the room to pour himself another shot of brandy. "Why don't you tell me the best way to handle a modern woman? A woman who doesn't really need a man."

She stared at him, perplexed. "I don't understand, Jarrett."

He leaned back against the wall and studied the brandy in his glass. "It's a simple enough question. And I freely admit I may not be the world's best at handling the female of the species. After all, I managed to blow my first marriage."

"I see." Hannah didn't, but she couldn't think of anything else to say.

"She was a modern woman. A beautiful, intelligent woman with a good career as the director of a museum. I met her when I first got into the art market. Elaine had everything. She didn't need men; she just used them. Used them to climb her way up to the directorship of a fine museum. Used them to obtain large foundation grants. Used

them to escort her to the best parties and the best places.
Used them to start her own private collection."

Hannah held her breath. "And in what ways did she use
you, Jarrett?"

His mouth twisted. "All of the above. I introduced her
to important and influential collectors. I helped her get
that directorship. I escorted her when she needed escort-
ing and I helped her obtain some very fine pieces for her
own collection. We were married for about a year and then
she met a far more important collector. One who had the
backing of a huge, privately endowed foundation. One
who moved in the best possible circles. She even used me
to get the introduction to him. And then she filed for a
divorce."

"Oh, Jarrett," Hannah whispered.

"I didn't threaten her, Hannah. I didn't lay down the
law. I played the role of the modern, supportive husband.
I helped her in every way I could. I agreed to hold off having children. I agreed to her extended, out-of-town business trips. Eventually I agreed to a divorce. No-fault
variety."

"And now you're afraid of making the same mistake
in handling me that you made in handling your ex-wife, is
that it? But it's not a question of *handling* people, Jarrett. It's a question of different kinds of personalities. You
can't make comparisons between me and your ex-wife.
We're two different women!"

He looked up from the golden brandy, and to her surprise he was smiling faintly. "That's what I decided in
Hawaii. I thought you were different. That you needed a
man. Specifically, that you needed me. Now I'm not so
sure. But one thing is still certain, God help me. I still want
you. Regardless of what kind of woman you are or
whether I learn to handle you properly, I want you." He
downed the last of his brandy and set the glass on a nearby

table. "So you're only getting two weeks of this crazy, sex-free affair. It's all I can stand. After that, if you're still here in my house we'll do things my way. Good night, Hannah."

He walked past her as she watched helplessly, then paused on the bottom step. "By the way. I have a rather unique security system set on the display cases. I turn it on at night. Don't ever try to get into the cases without making sure I've switched it off. Understand?" He climbed the stairs without waiting for an answer. A moment later a door closed behind him.

"Fantasy man. Fantasy man. Fantasy man."

"Shut up, Siegfried." Hannah roused herself from the sofa, found the birdcage cover, and silenced the parakeet by putting him to bed for the night. Beside her, Erasmus yawned. "I suppose it's time I let you out, isn't it?" Hannah noted.

She opened the door, and the dog trotted happily outside. Then she shut it behind him. It was nippy out there. Morosely she regarded the glass cases around her. "What am I doing here?" she asked herself again. She walked gingerly to the end of the room and surveyed the heavy volumes in the bookcase. "Not a thriller in the bunch. How dull."

But at the end of one shelf she found two with the name "J. Blade" on their spines. Overcome by curiosity, she pulled one of them down and flipped open the heavily bound cover. It appeared to be a discussion of certain aspects of Peruvian pre-Columbian art.

Maybe what she needed was a better understanding of the man she had fallen in love with, Hannah decided. And maybe there were some keys to be found in his writing. She lowered herself back onto the sofa and turned to the introductory chapter.

Twenty minutes later she roused herself from a discussion of the Chavín culture to let Erasmus inside. He settled down on the rug, and Hannah returned to the book.

Jarrett wrote very well, she was forced to acknowledge. In spite of her lack of interest in the topic, she found herself becoming fascinated with the tiny glimpses afforded into an ancient culture by its artifacts. Obviously, for Jarrett those glimpses were enough to inspire a lasting passion. The photographs of the sometimes charming, sometimes elegant, and sometimes grotesque art were beautifully arranged to complement the text. Slowly the sketchy story of great cultures unfolded.

It was after midnight when she turned a page to find a chapter on erotic pre-Columbian art. For a moment she was disconcerted by the unabashedly sexual aspect of the objects in the photographs and even more unnerved by Jarrett's accompanying text. She was certainly no prude, but somehow one expected a bit more prudery from such an ancient culture. On the other hand, Hannah decided with a grin, this aspect of art certainly underlined the consistency of human nature no matter what the era!

Jarrett's text seemed to acknowledge the fundamentally human quality of the artifacts. It treated the subject with both humor and respect. Hannah found herself admitting that there were more elemental human ties between a long-dead culture and the present than she would once have believed.

Reluctantly she closed the book halfway through and got to her feet with a wide yawn. The house seemed very quiet now. Erasmus and Siegfried and Herbie were all asleep. Yolanda and Ludmilla nodded in a corner near the window. No sounds had come from Jarrett's room for hours. It was time to go to bed.

Walking to the bookcase, Hannah replaced the volume she had been reading and turned to glance idly into the glass case nearby. Perhaps if she tried she might find something interesting in Jarrett's collection now that she had begun studying his book. She would be careful not to open the case.

But the first item that caught her eye wasn't in the glass case; it was sitting on top. It was the beautifully shaped shell she had found on the beach and given to Jarrett the night they baby-sat for little Danny.

Hannah's first reaction was one of disbelief. Slowly she picked it up and examined it. Jarrett had saved it. He'd actually carried the worthless little shell all the way home from Hawaii and found a place of honor for it near his priceless collection of ancient art. She could hardly believe it.

"Oh, Jarrett," she whispered, "maybe it's not so hopeless after all. Maybe you and I can find a way to make this relationship work. You must have felt something for me to make you save the shell. Something more than desire."

It was such a small thing on which to base so much hope.

Carefully Hannah set down the shell. Then she caught a familiar gleam of gold out of the corner of her eye. Instantly she froze.

She didn't want to acknowledge what she was seeing. Hannah stared at the statue under the glass and tried desperately to tell herself that the goddess she was looking at couldn't possibly be the same one that had caused her so much trouble in Hawaii.

But it was, and she knew it. The golden fertility goddess crouched now in Jarrett Blade's private collection. It had obviously never been returned to its rightful owner.

Jarrett had lied.

Nine

During the week that followed her arrival in Jarrett's home, Hannah felt as though she were walking a tightrope. At least three times each day she vowed she would confront him on the subject of the golden fertility goddess, and each time she lost her nerve.

She wasn't exactly certain why she lost her nerve. It had something to do with not wanting to have her worst suspicions confirmed, Hannah decided. If she pretended she'd never seen the goddess, she could go on pretending that Jarrett had been honest about what he intended to do with the statue. Maybe there was a perfectly legitimate explanation.

Maybe.

In the meantime she threw herself into creating a comfortable home out of the stuffy museum in which Jarrett lived. He watched the process with a kind of fascinated wariness. Occasionally he put his foot down.

"No, we are not moving that case full of textiles over by the window," he announced when she made known her intention to do so.

"But the colors in the cloth will be much more interesting in sunlight than over here in this dark corner with that funny lamp shining on them. We need some color over there, anyway."

"If you want color, put Siegfried over there. Not my textiles. The sunlight will fade them. Why the hell do you think I have them illuminated with that special lamp in the first place?"

"Oh. Well, how about that case of cute little pots? They'd look very nice over there standing under Yolanda and Ludmilla. In fact, we could plant some ferns in them. They'd made ideal planters!"

"Planters! My Nazca pots? Are you out of your mind? If you dare put one single fern in any of those pots, I'll stuff you into one!"

"Really, Jarrett, you don't have to get so emotional about them," Hannah declared huffily as she wielded a feather duster along a bookshelf. "I'm just trying to brighten the place up a bit."

There was a pause behind her as she stood on tiptoe to dust the top of one of his books. Then Jarrett stepped up behind her and encircled her waist with both of his strong hands. "Believe me, Hannah, you brighten this place up all by yourself," he told her roughly, dropping a quick kiss on the nape of her neck.

If she tried she could see the goddess out of the corner of her eye. Hannah steadfastly refused to glance at it. Instead she let herself enjoy the feel of Jarrett's hands on her waist. The duster froze in her hand.

"I...I've been reading one of the books you wrote," she confided in a tone she hoped was casual.

He nuzzled the curve of her shoulder. "Really? Did you find the section on erotic art?"

"Jarrett!" She flushed vividly, flustered.

"Want to see some prime examples? I've got some excellent pieces in that case over there by Herbie's bowl."

"Jarrett Blade!" And then Hannah's sense of humor got the better of her. "I suppose it does beat the old line about viewing your etchings," she giggled. "But I do wonder what it's doing to poor Herbie to have to be in such close proximity to that sort of thing."

"I don't think too much bothers Herbie." Jarrett released her. "What's for lunch?"

"Egg sandwiches. I thought we could take them down to the beach and have a picnic."

"Sounds great. I'll dig out some wine."

In spite of Jarrett's nervous complaints and cautions Hannah managed to rearrange his home to her satisfaction. She made him drive her to the local nursery so that she could purchase several more houseplants to keep Yolanda and Ludmilla company. She shifted the glass cases around so that they appeared more eclectically arranged not lined up museum-style. A few ferns draped over the top of the glass helped soften the formal look of the cases she discovered. Herbie and Siegfried and Erasmus also added comforting, cozy touches to the place. Hannah made certain that evening meals were accompanied by wine and candlelight and plenty of conversation, even though the discussions generally tended to be about pre-Columbian art. She replaced a couple of dark old paintings that Jarrett declared no interest in at all with mirrors strategically arranged to expand the ocean view and lighten the living room.

All in all, she and the animals had settled in very nicely by the end of the week. When he wasn't following her around, keeping an eye on her, Jarrett worked in his de outlining a new volume on Nazca pottery. Occasionally she heard him making phone calls during which he discussed pre-Columbian art and not much else. At least there were no phone calls to women, Hannah consoled herself.

But there were problems, too. For one thing there was the two-week deadline hanging over her head. Oh, she could leave easily enough before the two weeks were up, Hannah supposed, but she wasn't at all certain she'd have the willpower to do so when the time came. It was unfair of Jarrett to impose the deadline.

And there were the problems associated with the little golden goddess. Every time Hannah passed the case which contained the statue she gritted her teeth. Not only did the fertility goddess raise questions about Jarrett's business activities, she raised some rather personal questions as well. Each time Hannah passed the case that held the goddess, she found herself counting days. And every day now was another day too many.

"Damn you, if I'm pregnant I'm going to melt you down and turn you into a necklace," she hissed at the goddess toward the end of the week. The complication of pregnancy was all she needed, she told herself. There were so many things to be straightened out between herself and Jarrett. She'd always wanted a family, but she hadn't planned to start one in quite this fashion!

But the one factor that made her most anxious was the question of how Jarrett really felt toward her.

She thought she knew what he wanted from her now. He didn't appear to mind what she was doing to his house. He ate her food with relish. He seemed to enjoy the walks on the beach and he was genuinely fond of Herbie, Siegfried, and Erasmus. He was even polite to Yolanda and Ludmilla. Yes, Hannah told herself, he seemed to want the comfortable, cozy home she was trying to create.

And he wanted her in his bed.

There was no doubt now in her mind that Jarrett Blad
had been a lonely, self-contained man for most of his life
He wanted affection, even love, although the only way h
knew how to ask for it was in a high-handed, brusquel
arrogant style.

But he was also deeply wary of making a woman hi
equal, his partner in a relationship. Jarrett had to have th
security of being needed. He wanted to know that she de
pended on him. It was the only way he could feel certai
of her.

Yes, she was beginning to understand what he wanted
But Hannah wasn't at all certain of what he had to offe
in return.

At the end of the first week Hannah took special pain
with dinner.

"Our first anniversary?" Jarrett joked as he surveye
the grilled salmon with lemon butter and the hot spinac
salad.

Hannah felt a little goaded by the remark. "Why not
There may never be another."

He looked up, the humor fading from his eyes. "Yo
mean you might not be here at the end of next week?"

She couldn't quite face the directness of the question
"If I am it will be your turn to cook the anniversary din
ner," she mumbled, reaching for her chilled Chardonna
wine.

"It will be my pleasure since I'll know I'll be having yo
for dessert," he drawled.

"You're deliberately trying to bait me," she accused.

He shrugged. "Perhaps. Maybe I don't like this perio
of uncertainty any better than you do."

"I'm getting by just fine!"

"Well, I'm not. I lie in bed at night and think of hov
you would look lying in my arms. I dream of undressin
you and carrying you naked up the stairs to my bedroom

wake up needing a cold shower in the middle of the night.
spend countless hours planning ways to seduce you when
he two weeks are over.''

"I had no idea sex occupied so much of a man's think-
ng!'' Hannah tossed back spiritedly. "It's amazing the
male of the species has so much time for earning a living
or making war or playing golf!''

"We're a versatile lot.''

"So are women,'' she shot back smoothly. "Which is
why modern women don't take kindly to being confined to
he bedroom and the kitchen. It's why they want and need
a few more opportunities and choices in life.''

"Are we going to argue on our first anniversary?'' Jarrett murmured.

Hannah sighed. "I give up. You really won't discuss it,
will you?''

"Anything else but the changing role of the family,'' he
quipped, giving her one of his rarest, most charming
smiles. "I have a question for you, though, on a related
subject.''

She eyed him suspiciously. "Yes?''

"Why haven't you ever married? There must be plenty
of men around who would be more than happy to give you
he kind of marriage you want.''

"What kind of marriage do you think I want, Jarrett?'' she countered earnestly.

He hesitated. "You've implied you want a modern arrangement. Lots of independence. No strong economic
ties. No dependence on a man. A partnership with sex.''

"That's not quite what I want,'' she told him carefully.
"I want love, too.''

He shrugged and cut into the perfect salmon fillet.
"Love, too,'' he agreed casually. "So why haven't you
gotten what you wanted?''

Hannah felt a sense of helplessness. He didn't under
stand. "I thought I was going to get it once," she tried to
say lightly. "I was in love with a man who offered me all
of the things I wanted. Or so I believed at the time."

Jarrett watched her closely. "What happened?"

"He used me to get something he wanted more than he
wanted me."

"What was that?"

"A look at some classified company documents I was in
charge of indexing and filing."

Jarrett stared at her. "You're kidding!" He looked
dumbfounded.

"Nope. We indexers handle all the critical files and pa
pers in a company. We have access to everything." She
could smile about it now. "Don't look at me like that. At
least he didn't leave me for another woman!"

"What did he leave you for?"

"Another job after he got fired," she admitted wryly.
"I never saw him again."

"Did he get what he wanted from you?" Jarrett de
manded coolly.

"No. He wasn't a very good company spy, I'm afraid. I
realized before it was too late exactly what he was after.
When I told him I couldn't possibly give him the papers
he tried to get them himself and got caught by his
supervisor."

"And after him?" Jarrett asked.

"No one else has offered me quite what I want," she
confessed gently. "There have been other men who have
asked me to marry them, but somehow it's never felt quite
right. Something's always been missing."

"What's been missing?"

"You're certainly full of questions tonight," she chided.

He waved the interruption aside. "What's been miss
ing, Hannah?"

"I'm not sure, to tell you the truth. Sometimes the package contains all the ingredients but the resulting offer leaves me cold. I can't explain it. I just know something's always been missing."

"Are you sure you really know what you want?' Jarrett asked softly.

She stared at him in astonishment, about to answer with definite "yes." And then Hannah realized she was stumbling over the single word. "Perhaps not," she admitted. "At least, perhaps not in the past. But I do now."

She wanted Jarrett Blade. In whatever capacity she could have him. Hannah knew that now with boundless certainty.

Jarrett saw the certainty in her eyes and felt chilled. Everything had been so much simpler when he'd been sure she needed him to look after her. But the soft, gentle woman he'd encountered in Hawaii had an underlying strength that made it clear she could survive quite well without him. His frustration grew as he considered the fact that the only hold he seemed to have on her was a physical one—and she'd made him swear not to use it.

"Is something wrong, Jarrett?" Hannah frowned in concern from the opposite side of the table. "Is the fish bad?"

"The fish is perfect."

"You look a little strange."

"I'm contemplating the fact that most couples celebrating their first week's anniversary generally go to bed together after dinner," he growled.

"Oh." She suddenly became very busy serving him a second helping of spinach salad. "Well, we're not most couples, are we? Some more sourdough bread, Jarrett?"

"Some more wine, I think," he drawled, reaching for the bottle.

The evening deteriorated after that. Hannah became increasingly nervous as Jarrett polished off the bottle of wine. By the time he'd eaten her chocolate mousse, she was positively agitated.

He helped her clear the dishes and then insisted they top off the dinner with a brandy in front of the fire. Hannah agreed, but he could see the hesitancy in her. It annoyed him, so he poured himself a double when he poured the brandies.

He was on his second double and conversation appeared to have stopped altogether when he finally demanded an explanation.

"Why are you looking like a scared rabbit, Hannah?"

She lowered her lashes and gazed into the fire. "Probably because you're starting to look like a drunk wolf."

"I am not drunk," he stated categorically. Was he? she wondered.

"If you say so. Look, Jarrett, it's rather late. I think I'll go to bed. We can do the dishes in the morning." She got to her feet and moved away from the sofa.

"We're supposed to be getting to know each other," he complained. "How can we do that if you're always running off?"

"I am not always running off. We can talk in the morning, if you like."

He eyed her intently from beneath hooded lashes. She was standing uncertainly at the far end of the sofa like a small, wild creature that doesn't know whether to freeze or run. Jarrett deliberately leaned back into his corner of the sofa, one leg resting on the cushions, the other foot on the floor.

"Don't rush off, honey," he murmured. "Don't be afraid of me."

Her eyes flashed resentfully. "I am not afraid of you, Jarrett. If I were, I wouldn't have come here to stay with

ou. I wouldn't have trusted your word of honor when you
agreed to my terms.''

"Did I give my word?'' he inquired vaguely, honestly
trying to recall the conversation.

"You certainly did!''

"I see. But I also put a limit on this idiotic situation,
didn't I?''

"Two weeks. This is only the end of the first. Jarrett,
'm going upstairs to bed.''

"That sounds lovely. You run along and I'll see to the
fire. Then I'll go on upstairs myself.'' He smiled blandly.
Hannah did not appear to find the expression reassuring.
She frowned and edged toward the staircase.

"Jarrett?''

"Umm?'' He glanced at the fire, idly checking the state
of the glowing coals. They were dying down safely. He
would just pull the screen closed and that would be that.

"Jarrett, what are you going to do?''

"I told you. Take care of the fire and then go upstairs to
bed.'' Deliberately he smiled again.

"Stop that!'' she suddenly snapped, her hand on the
newel post.

"Stop what?''

"Stop undressing me with your eyes. Dammit, Jarrett,
you've had too much to drink.''

"Would you rather I undressed you with my hands?'' he
asked whimsically.

"No!''

"Don't tell fibs, honey. You know I could make you
happy tonight. Why wait another week? What are you
going to know about me a week from now that you don't
know tonight?'' He sat up slowly so as not to startle her
into full flight up the staircase. Industriously he grabbed
a poker and played a bit with the coals in the fire.

"Jarrett, you need to go to bed and sleep it off. You're drunk."

"You sound disapproving." He slanted her a sidelong glance, studying the way she was now clutching the newel post. "And you look disapproving," he added with a flickering smile. "You can look so damned sweet and regal at the same time. How do you manage that? Maybe it's the way you wear your hair in that crown. I think I prefer your hair down. When it's flowing around your shoulders you don't look so aloof and disapproving. You look like a woman waiting for her man."

Hannah climbed two of the steps, her eyes never leaving his face. Jarrett knew a sense of fierce anticipation. The chase was on. Her flight was still disguised as a casual attempt to climb the stairs, but they both knew she was running now. Slowly he set down the poker and got to his feet. The room spun briefly around him, and he found that annoying. Automatically his hand went out to steady himself on the arm of the sofa.

Hannah climbed another step, her eyes very wide and questioning in the shadowy light. "Jarrett, no..."

"Jarrett, yes," he drawled softly, risking a step away from the support of the sofa. Sheer, driving male need seemed to be doing a fair job of keeping him on his feet and headed in the right direction. The whole world narrowed down to the distance between himself and Hannah.

"Jarrett, don't you dare," she whispered, putting another stair tread between them as he stalked cautiously to the foot of the steps. She was about halfway up now, and the expression in her eyes was also about halfway. Halfway between anger and pure fear.

Talk to her, Jarrett told himself wisely, talk to her while you close in. It will distract her. "Hannah, don't be afraid of me."

She licked her lips. "You told me once a little fear wouldn't hurt," she reminded him accusingly.

He shook his head. "That first time I made love to you? So I did. Did you know what I meant at the time? I only wanted you to realize that what we had between us was nothing casual. I wanted you to think about the full implications of what we were doing. I wanted you to look into my eyes and know you might get pregnant. I wanted you to cling to me and know at the same time that I wouldn't let you run to safety when it was all over. I wanted you *aware* of me, Hannah. On every level. There's nothing like a bit of fear to make a woman aware of a man. Especially a woman like you."

"You really are drunk," she whispered, inching up another stair although he hadn't yet started his ascent. "How many glasses of wine did you have?"

"Not enough. The double brandies helped a bit, however. And then there was that whiskey on the rocks I fixed before dinner. Actually"—he broke off reflectively—"it's getting a little difficult to remember exactly."

"An excellent reason for calling a halt to this seduction scene," she shot back. "What's the point of trying to pounce on me if you won't be able to remember what happened in the morning?"

He grinned at her, making no attempt to modify what must surely have been a wicked, wholly male expression of sensual anticipation. "As soon as I wake up with you in my arms, I'm sure everything will come back to me." He put one foot on the bottom stair and saw still greater tension stiffen her soft, curving body. "There's no point waiting another week, Hannah, and we both know it. I want you. And when I have you in my arms I can make you want me. I can make you *need* me. Are you going to run, or are you going to accept the inevitable gracefully?"

"Damn you, Jarrett Blade! I'm not going to let you touch me! You gave me your word!"

Hannah broke and ran, fleeing up the staircase like a startled doe before the hunter. Jarrett watched the pleasant shape of her derriere as she darted around the post at the top of the stairs and then, smiling with grim intent, he started after her.

There was no point in running, and in all honesty Jarrett had to admit he probably would have fallen flat on his face if he'd tried. This sort of thing took care when a man was not entirely sober. So he stalked up the stairs with slow, steady deliberation, knowing his quarry couldn't escape.

At the top of the stairs he paused for a moment to let the walls stop whirling and then he started in the direction of Hannah's bedroom. *His* bedroom, Jarrett corrected himself coolly. He owned this house, didn't he?

Her door was closed, naturally. Probably locked, too. But that didn't make any difference. The locks in this house were simple, ineffective mechanisms, except for the ones he had installed on the outside windows and doors. The ones on inside doors were meant only to remind people of privacy requirements. As the owner of the house, he didn't need to pay any attention, Jarrett assured himself. He raised a hand and twisted the knob. It didn't give.

"Open the door, Hannah," he ordered softly.

"Go away, Jarrett!"

"We both know I'm not going to go away. Open the door, honey, or I'll break the lock."

There was no response from Hannah, but his ears caught the unmistakable sound of a heavy piece of furniture being pushed or pulled across the floor. Was she trying to move the dresser in front of the door? Dammit, that would be a rather effective barrier! He'd have to act quickly, before she could shove the dresser into place.

Standing back, he gathered his senses and his energy with a supreme effort of will and slashed out with his foot in a swift, savage kick that burst the lock and shoved open the door.

For an instant he simply stood, bracing himself against the doorjamb with one hand. Trying to practice karate when drunk was a tricky business. Now the room was really spinning.

"Damn!" he snarled under his breath, fighting to regain his equilibrium. Then he saw Hannah standing with her back to the window on the other side of the room. He shook his head and took a step forward. "Like a little goddess," he muttered, forced to admire her disdainful, royal pose. "Are you going to use your judo, sweetheart? You didn't that first night in Hawaii. I wonder why."

"Leave me alone, Jarrett," she commanded haughtily.

"Can't leave you alone. That's the whole problem." He closed the distance between them. "Only place I can be sure of you is in bed, so that's where we're going. Are you going to fight me?"

"Yes," she bit out savagely.

"Won't do any good," he advised her complacently. "Whenever I touch you, you melt."

"Not tonight, Jarrett."

"Why not tonight?" He reached a point only a foot or so away from her and stood looking down at his captive. Almost experimentally he put out a hand and touched the coronet of her hair. She flinched, but she didn't move.

"You gave me your word, Jarrett," she reminded him, her aqua eyes suddenly very cool and steady.

"I was a fool."

"It doesn't make any difference. You promised me two weeks. I came to you because you gave me your word that you wouldn't try to push me into bed."

His jaw tightened as he resisted the argument. Dammit, he didn't have to listen to that sort of thing tonight. This was his house, his woman, and he could do as he pleased. Besides, there was no other way to hold Hannah, was there? His fingers dug luxuriously into her hair, tugging free the braids.

"Hannah..."

"Go away, Jarrett. I'm going to sleep alone tonight."

His fist closed around one braid and he angrily pulled her face close to his own. He watched her, feeling as if he were on fire and wondering why the force of the blaze didn't singe her. "I could take you so easily tonight, Hannah."

She licked her dry lower lip. "You won't. You promised."

"There's no one here to enforce that stupid promise!"

"You're here," she pointed out very levelly.

"Christ, Hannah, I'd be a fool not to take you to bed. Don't you understand?" Why was he trying to explain it to her? Talk about idiocy. It must be the liquor in him.

"Go to your own room, Jarrett. I'll still be here in the morning."

"No, you won't. You'll run again, won't you? Just like you did that time in Hawaii. I can't let you run again."

"Why should I run tomorrow?" she asked with gentle logic. "I've already been here a week, and I'm planning to stay for at least another week."

He shut his eyes and then opened them to stare down at her in bemused fury. "You'll run because in the morning you'll tell yourself you can't trust me," he finally explained heavily. "And you'll be right."

She said nothing, looking up at him with an unreadable expression in her eyes. What the devil was she thinking? he wondered. That she already knew she couldn't trust him because of his behavior this evening? A helpless rage

threatened to overwhelm him, and then, exercising every
ounce of strength he possessed, he released her and stepped
back.

"Go to bed, Hannah," he snarled. "Go to bed and plot
your safe return to your safe, serene, cozy little cottage in
Seattle where your good job and your good friends are all
waiting. Go to bed and plan your return to your pleasant
lifestyle. Find some man who is happy to have a room-
mate relationship with you. One who will go halves on
everything. A real *partner*. And when it's all over the two
of you can get a no-fault divorce! Just like a couple of
partners breaking up a small business arrangement!"

Turning so quickly that he had to catch himself on the
edge of the bed, Jarrett headed for the door. There was silence behind him, but he didn't dare look back as he managed to make the hall and then the stairs.

An inner anger unlike anything he had ever known
seized him as he stalked back downstairs to the living
room. What a fool he was. He'd blown everything tonight. A damned fool!

Savagely he grabbed the brandy bottle, not even bothering with the nearby glass. He wasn't feeling civilized
enough for a glass tonight. Throwing himself down on the
sofa, he took a long swallow of the fiery liquor.

A fool. She'd leave in the morning, of course, just as
he'd predicted. Why in hell had he let his growing fear get
the better of him tonight? But that was exactly what had
happened. His fear that he wouldn't be able to hold her
had actually driven her away!

Jarrett lifted the brandy bottle to his lips again.

It was the sound of Erasmus barking his familar warning that roused Hannah from a restless sleep the next
morning. It took several moments for the noise to regis-

ter, and by the time it did she realized it had already stopped. Jarrett must have answered the door.

It occurred to her that in the week she had been staying at his house they hadn't had any visitors. Jarrett Blade was not the sociable type. Voices drifted up from the floor below as she tugged on her jeans and a wide-sleeved shirt with narrow cuffs. There was something familiar about those voices....

Hastily Hannah bound her hair up into the usual braided coronet and slid her feet into sandals. Then she opened the door and listened intently.

The voices in the room below belonged to John and Alice Clydemore. Hannah went very still with shock.

"Well, well, Blade," John Clydemore was saying almost jovially, "so there she is. Safe and sound in your fine collection. An excellent addition to it, if I might say so."

"Get to the point, Clydemore. Why are you here?" Jarrett's voice sounded weary and dulled, as if he were fighting with chronic pain. No doubt a severe headache brought on by last night's drinking, Hannah thought.

She moved silently to the edge of the landing and glanced down. John and Alice Clydemore were standing very much at ease in Jarrett's living room. Alice was gazing appreciatively at the collection of Nazca pots and John was studying the golden goddess as she crouched in the glass case. Jarrett, arms folded across his bare chest and wearing only his dark khaki slacks, propped up a wall and watched his visitors with a cold expression. He looked vicious. And he looked as if he really did have a headache.

"Come now, Jarrett, dear," Alice chuckled richly, "as soon as we found out the goddess hadn't gone back to Señor Valesquez's collection, we knew exactly what had happened to her. Couldn't resist her, could you? Of course not. Who could? Don't blame you in the least. But you're also a wily dealer, my friend, and what John and I have to offer is the deal of a lifetime. We have a buyer.''

"Tell your buyer to go to hell."

"Tell Dominic Arlington to go to hell?" John Clydemore drawled. "I think not."

"Arlington!" The muffled explosion of his words was accompanied by a low groan. Hannah saw Jarrett's hand go briefly to his head. Then, as if regretting the visible sign of weakness, he set his jaw and recrossed his arms.

"That's right. Arlington. He'll pay a fortune, Blade," John said coolly. "No questions asked. He wants her. Badly."

"She's not for sale." Jarrett's voice was much lower this time, and Hannah had to strain to hear it.

"Everything is for sale in this business. You know that," Alice murmured. "The three of us can set our price. Arlington will meet it. He's already made that very clear."

"And that's why you're here? To form a partnership with me?" Jarrett moved, and Hannah realized he was walking into the kitchen. "What about what happened in Hawaii? No hard feelings?"

"Business is business," John explained equably. "If you're fixing coffee, I'll have some too."

Coffee! Hannah stared down at the three people as they trooped into the kitchen. Jarrett was going to fix coffee while they all calmly discussed the illegal sale of the goddess? She caught her breath and then started downstairs, the carpeted treads making no sound under her sandals. Just what did Jarrett think he was doing? He had other things to consider now. He was no longer free to make questionable deals in pre-Columbian antiquities!

Head high, eyes gleaming with her determination, Hannah swung around the corner of the kitchen doorway and found John and Alice seated at the table. With a careful precision which told of his aching head, Jarrett was measuring coffee into the drip pot.

"Well, if it isn't little Hannah Prescott." Alice Clyde-more smiled graciously. "I was just about to ask Jarrett whatever had become of you. I gather he found you amusing enough for a short affair, hmm?"

"Shut up, Alice," Jarrett interrupted flatly, staring at Hannah. "Hannah, I think you'd better go back upstairs."

"Upstairs! Not on your life!" she gritted.

Jarrett drew a long, patient breath. "This doesn't concern you."

"Like hell it doesn't! What do you think you're doing, Jarrett Blade?"

"Your friend Blade is about to become a very wealthy man, my dear." John settled comfortably back in his chair and regarded her with his amused, patrician gaze.

"By selling that stupid goddess? Not a chance. That goddess belongs to Jorge Valesquez and it's going back to him very soon. *Isn't it, Jarrett?*" she asked, whirling on him in challenge.

He blinked at her like a large, still-sleepy cat. "It is?"

"It most certainly is," she declared. "Mr. and Mrs. Clydemore, you might as well get up and leave right now. Jarrett will not be participating in any more shady deals. That goddess is going back where she belongs, and Jarrett will continue to earn his living by writing books and doing appraisals and brokering *legitimate* deals. Is that very clear?"

"Oh, it's clear enough," Alice said politely. "But I'm afraid it's not entirely accurate. You know nothing about these things, Hannah. Jarrett's right. Go back upstairs and wait for him in bed. That's your role in his life, isn't it? There's more money involved here than you can possibly imagine. Stay out of it."

"Hannah!" Jarrett's voice sliced like a whip across the kitchen. "Go upstairs."

"Not on your life! You're not going to treat me like a naive little idiot who just happened to stumble into the wrong scene and get in everyone's way. *You are speaking to the mother of your child.*"

The cup in Jarrett's fingers slipped from his grasp and fell to the floor. He didn't appear to notice. He was staring at Hannah in utter astonishment.

"What did you say?" he said a little thickly.

"I'm pregnant," she told him boldly. "That means that you now have a family, Jarrett Blade. This family of yours requires a man who will be both father and husband. It requires a man who knows the meaning of responsibility. You are responsible now for me and for your baby. We need a stable home and a man we can depend on. Responsible fathers do not conduct shady business deals," she concluded sweetly.

"Oh, for God's sake, Jarrett, get rid of her, will you?" John Clydemore sounded impatient and bored at the same time.

"He can't get rid of me. I belong to him and I need him. He has no time now to get involved with people like you. You two are the ones who will have to leave. The sooner the better. Jarrett and I have plans to make for our family."

"Blade, I'm warning you. Hannah is becoming something of a nuisance. I'm sure she's fine in bed, but she obviously doesn't have much of a head for business. Get rid of her." John Clydemore glowered at Hannah.

Hannah ignored him and walked serenely across the room to stand looking up at Jarrett, who was watching her with an intensity that might have been frightening under other circumstances. Delicately she put her hand on his arm and smiled.

"You don't get involved in these sorts of deals any-more, do you, darling? The goddess will be going back to her rightful owner, won't she?"

"You sound very certain of that," he rasped.

"Of course I am," Hannah said gently. "I trust you implicitly. And you've told me that you're not in this end of the business these days. Even if you were, it would be time to leave the unscrupulous side of things behind."

He swallowed heavily, gunmetal-gray eyes gleaming with a fire that warmed her. "Because I have a family to take care of now?"

She nodded. "Precisely. This sort of deal would set a bad example for the children, wouldn't it? Not to men-tion how nervous it would make their mother. I'm a little old-fashioned in some ways, Jarrett, my love. I expect my husband to make his living in a reasonably honest fashion."

"Your husband?" he breathed.

"And in return for everything he will do for me, I am willing to love, honor, and, within reason, obey." She smiled tenderly, her eyes shining with a hint of laughter and a great deal of love. "I'm not saying I'll do what you say one hundred percent of the time, but I am saying I re-spect you and trust you enough to put myself and our baby in your keeping. You are the man of the family, darling. I need you," she concluded simply.

Jarrett groaned huskily and pulled her into his arms. "Hannah..."

"Well, I must say this is all very touching, if a little cloying at this hour of the morning," John Clydemore announced in a new, harder tone of voice, "but I'm af-riad Alice and I don't have time for the drama."

Hannah glanced at him and then, startled by the gun in his hand, she stepped back a pace from Jarrett's hold. Be-side her, Jarrett turned.

"What the hell do you think you're doing, Clyde-more?" Jarrett asked far too softly.

"John and I came for the goddess," Alice explained coolly. "We intend to get her one way or another. The sensible thing is to deal. But if you won't deal, then I'm afraid we will have to take more direct measures. Hannah, go and fetch the goddess out of the case."

"Fetch her yourself," Jarrett snapped, his hand going out to take hold of Hannah's shoulder before she could move.

"Credit us with some intelligence, Blade," John Clydemore said easily. "Everyone knows you take care of your collection. Gossip has it that a person could lose a hand sticking it into one of those cases without your express permission."

"Don't be ridiculous," Jarrett retorted wearily. "All you have to do is open the case and lift out the goddess. Those cases aren't booby-trapped."

"Then you won't object if Hannah does the fetching and carrying, will you? After all, no harm will come to her, will it?"

"Just take the thing and go," Jarrett said, his hand still on Hannah's shoulder. She could feel his fingers digging into her flesh with abnormal strength. Worriedly she slid a sideways glance up at him.

John Clydemore waved the gun meaningfully. "Hannah, get the goddess or I'll take one of his legs out from under him."

"Hannah, wait!" Jarrett spoke urgently as she instantly slipped away from his grasp.

She halted, turning to glance back at him uneasily. "Yes, Jarrett?"

He ran a hand through his tousled brown hair, and his mouth crooked wryly. "Make sure the switch on the side of the bookcase is flipped to the off position."

Hannah nodded uncertainly. "The off position."

"Make sure, Hannah," he stated evenly.

"Yes, Jarrett." Quickly she turned back, heading for the case that contained the goddess. She passed it first, located the small switch on the bookcase, a switch she had never noticed before, and quickly switched it to the off position. Then she went back for the goddess. Through the kitchen doorway she could see Alice Clydemore keeping an eye on her while her husband held the gun on Jarrett.

"You've been nothing but trouble, lady," Hannah muttered to the round, golden deity as she lifted it out of the case with both hands. "You should have stayed buried back in Peru. On the other hand, I suppose I never would have met Jarrett if it hadn't been for you. Come on. Those two in there deserve you."

Clutching the gold statue, Hannah carried it back to the kitchen and paused in the doorway.

"Ah, excellent. Hand her over, Hannah." Much pleased, Alice Clydemore stepped forward to collect the statue.

It was now or never, Hannah told herself resolutely. "Here you go, Clydemore," she called out to the man with the gun. "Catch!" Without pause she hurled the heavy goddess straight at John Clydemore, relying on the instincts of a connoisseur, the same kind of instincts that had made Jarrett reach out to catch the statue the night she had thrown it at his head.

A man who was so wrapped up in his passion for artifacts of the long-dead past didn't do the logical thing like step aside when a golden statue came hurtling toward him. He dropped everything to catch it. Instinctively.

Alice Clydemore screamed as her husband fumbled with the gun in his frantic effort to catch the statue.

"Damn you!" he hissed. The gun went flying at the same time that the golden goddess struck his grasping

and. But what sent the gun arcing toward the kitchen wall
as the impact made by Jarrett's bare foot when it struck
lydemore's arm with a terrifying crack.

There was a cry of pain and rage from Clydemore as he
opped to his knees, holding his arm protectively against
s chest. Alice Clydemore turned on the source of the di-
ster, leaping for Hannah with outstretched, clawing
ngers.

Hannah barely had time to find her balance. An instant
ter the infuriated woman was upon her. Hannah caught
r behind the elbow, pivoted on her foot, and used the
oman's savage momentum against her. A split-second
ter Alice fell full length upon the kitchen floor and lay
ere groaning.

"Hannah, are you all right?"

Hannah glanced up from her victim to see Jarrett with
e gun in his hand. He looked a bit too familiar with the
eapon, she decided. Then she saw the goddess lying on
e floor under the kitchen table.

"I'm fine. I hope that stupid statue is still in one piece."

"Forget it," Jarrett ordered irritably. "Get away from
rs. Clydemore. Come over here and call the sheriff's
epartment. The number's on the inside of the phone
ook. Are you sure you're all right? You didn't hurt
urself? The baby..."

"I'm sure the baby will take after his father and be a
rdy little soul." Hannah smiled as she stepped across the
om to pick up the phone. "Probably be born knowing
e rudiments of karate."

Jarrett smiled very slowly. "Or judo."

"Or judo," she agreed, dialing the number on the in-
le of the directory.

It was several hours later before Hannah and Jarrett
und themselves alone once more in the house. The sher-

iff had come and gone mumbling something about straightforward case against the Clydemores. John an Alice, looking far less patrician than when they had a rived, had been led off in handcuffs. Siegfried, Erasmus and Herbie had all finally calmed down.

"Not that Herbie ever did appear particularly alarmed, Hannah exclaimed as she sat on the sofa and eyed the tu tle fondly.

"Handsome Siegfried. Handsome Siegfried. Hand some Siegfried."

"Yes, I know, Siegfried, you're very handsome," Han nah soothed.

Jarrett ignored the pets and sank down beside Hannah folding her close. His eyes were deep pools of hunger tha had nothing at all to do with simple desire. It went far b yond that.

"Are you sure, Hannah?"

She smiled up at him, relaxing in his arms. "About th baby? I'm sure. It's what comes of hanging out aroun fertility goddesses, I imagine. We shall have to be ver careful in the future."

"That particular fertility goddess won't be around her much longer," Jarrett told her steadily. "She's going bac to Jorge Valesquez."

"I know."

"You do?" He eyed her searchingly.

"Oh, yes. I know. You've said she was going back to h rightful owner, and I trust you completely."

Jarrett appeared to have trouble finding the right word Then his mouth softened in a rare smile. "Thank yo sweetheart. I won't let you down. The real truth is that sh was going back to Valesquez all along. After I brought th statue back from Hawaii he told me to keep it in my co lection until he paid his next visit to the States. He's du sometime next month. He'll be our houseguest."

"That's nice."

"You really believe me?"

"Of course I do. I wouldn't marry a man I didn't trust."
annah realized even as she spoke the words that they
ere nothing less than the truth. She trusted Jarrett Blade
d she always had.

"Last night," he began awkwardly, his eyes darkening.
Last night I thought I'd ruined everything."

"You got a little drunk and a little impatient." Hannah
inned. "I shall have to see to it that you don't have cause
do either again in the future."

"You're going to marry me?"

"Didn't I just stand in the kitchen and propose not three
urs ago?"

"Definitely."

"Are you willing to have me for a wife?"

"Hannah, I'm going to marry you as soon as it's le-
lly possible," he assured her gravely. "I'm not taking
y more chances. I'm going to take care of you and the
by. I'll make you happy."

"Yes, Jarrett," she agreed equably, trailing her fingers
rough the hair on the nape of his neck. "I have every
nfidence in you as a husband and as a father."

He frowned. "About your decision to work..."

"We can discuss it later. Much later."

"No, I want to tell you now that it's all right with me, if
at's what you want."

"You're not afraid of a working wife?" she teased
ntly.

"I'm not afraid in our case. With you, your husband
d your children will always come first, won't they?"

"Always. When you've waited as long as I have to ob-
n a family, you have your priorities firmly in
rspective."

He nodded. "I know. I've waited even longer. You ar our children will always be my first priority. Do you b lieve me?"

"Yes."

"I love you, Hannah."

"I know." She smiled wistfully.

"How do you know?" he demanded, brushing h mouth lightly with his own.

"I knew when the goddess was lying flat on her ba under the kitchen table where I had thrown her and y ignored her completely to find out if I was all right, Hannah explained complacently.

Jarrett looked momentarily startled; then he grinne "To tell you the truth, I honestly didn't give her a thoug at the time. All I could think about was you."

"True love."

"Must be." His grin faded into a far more inte expression. "Yes, it definitely is. Hannah, I haver wanted to admit that what I felt for you was love, a though I should have known it when I found myse agreeing to your stupid plan to get to know one another a sex-free affair. I was scared to death I wouldn't be ab to hold you without the sex. And after I blew everythin last night..."

"I still would have been here for our second annive sary next week," she assured him laughingly. "But to t you the truth, I decided last night to put everything ontc more normal footing today."

"Normal footing? Does that mean you were going start a real affair with me?"

"I'm afraid so." She sighed. "You see, I realized la night that there really wasn't anything more I had to lea about you. I knew I loved you. That was all th mattered."

"What about all the things you wanted me to learn? That stuff about a partnership between us and the modern approach to marriage and the changing role of women in society?" He looked worried again, and Hannah lifted her fingers to smooth the lines in his face.

"Jarrett, darling, I think we're going to have to face the fact that you are a little old-fashioned in some ways." She smiled demurely. "Some might even say primitive. But that's all right, because I appear to have a bit of the primitive in me, too. I suspect that's what's been missing from my previous associations with the male of the species. I need a man who understands the fundamental things in life. Understands and respects them. A lot of modern men don't."

His mouth curved in wry amusement. "You're saying I'm not a modern sort of male?"

"Are you?"

"No. No, I guess not. I've always felt a bit out of it, to tell you the truth. As if I didn't quite fit into the twentieth century somehow."

"And now?"

"Now," he drawled, lowering his mouth to within an inch of hers, "everything seems just right. I've found my missing goddess. The one who needs me and loves me as much as I need and love her. It wouldn't matter what century we found ourselves in. The relationship between you and me will always be a little on the primitive side. Hannah?"

"Hmm?"

"Why didn't you ever use your judo against me?"

"I couldn't seem to think properly whenever you got that close," she admitted with a rueful grin. "At first you were a fantasy come to life, and a dangerous one at that. I couldn't figure out how to deal with it. Then I realized I was falling in love with you. I could hardly use judo against you when all I wanted was to be in your arms.''

Jarrett's mouth curved in satisfaction. He brushed her lips tantalizingly with his own. ''Remember the quilt I bought in Hawaii?''

''Yes.''

''It's waiting for us upstairs on my bed.''

''Yes.''

Safe once more in the glass case, the golden goddess of fertility watched with wise, ancient eyes as two members of the modern generation climbed the stairs to rediscover some very old truths about the relationship between men and women.

READERS' COMMENTS ON SILHOUETTE DESIRES

"Thank you for Silhouette Desires. They are the best thing that has happened to the bookshelves in a long time."

—V.W.*, Knoxville, TN

"Silhouette Desires—wonderful, fantastic—the best romance around."

—H.T.*, Margate, N.J.

"As a writer as well as a reader of romantic fiction, I found DESIREs most refreshingly realistic—and definitely as magical as the love captured on their pages."

—C.M.*, Silver Lake, N.Y.

"I just wanted to let you know how very much I enjoy your Silhouette Desire books. I read other romances, and I must say your books rate up at the top of the list."

—C.N.*, Anaheim, CA

"Desires are number one. I especially enjoy the endings because they just don't leave you with a kiss or embrace; they finish the story. Thank you for giving me such reading pleasure."

—M.S.*, Sandford, FL

*names available on request

You won't want to miss a single one of the heart-felt stories presented by Silhouette Special Edition; and when you take advantage of this special offer, you won't have to.

You'll also receive a FREE subscription to the Silhouette Books Newsletter as long as you remain a member. Each lively issue is filled with news on upcoming titles, interviews with your favorite authors, even their favorite recipes.

To become a home subscriber and receive your first 4 books FREE, fill out and mail the coupon today!

Silhouette Special Edition®

Silhouette Books, 120 Brighton Rd., P.O. Box 5084, Clifton, NJ 07015-5084

Take 4 Silhouette
Intimate Moments novels
FREE

Then preview 4 brand new Silhouette Intimate Moments® novels
—delivered to your door every month—for 15 days as soon as
they are published. When you decide to keep them, you pay just
$2.25 each ($2.50 each, in Canada), *with no shipping, handling, or other charges of any kind!*

Silhouette Intimate Moments novels are not for everyone.
They were created to give you a more detailed, more exciting
reading experience, filled with romantic fantasy, intense sensuality, and stirring passion.

The first 4 Silhouette Intimate Moments novels are absolutely
FREE and without obligation, yours to keep. You can cancel at
any time.

You'll also receive a FREE subscription to the Silhouette Books
Newsletter as long as you remain a member. Each issue is filled
with news on upcoming titles, interviews with your favorite
authors, even their favorite recipes.

To get your 4 FREE books, fill out and mail the coupon today!

Silhouette Intimate Moments®

Silhouette Books, 120 Brighton Rd., P.O. Box 5084, Clifton, NJ 07015-5084

Clip and mail to: Silhouette Books,
120 Brighton Road, P.O. Box 5084, Clifton, NJ 07015-5084 *

YES. Please send me 4 FREE Silhouette Intimate Moments novels. Unless you
hear from me after I receive them, send me 4 brand new Silhouette Intimate
Moments novels to preview each month. I understand you will bill me just $2.25
each, a total of $9.00 (in Canada, $2.50 each, a total of $10.00)—with no
shipping, handling, or other charges of any kind. There is no minimum number
of books that I must buy, and I can cancel at any time. The first 4 books are mine
to keep. *Silhouette Intimate Moments available in Canada through subscription only.*

IM-SUB-1   **BM1826**

Name _____ (please print)

Address _____ Apt. #

City _____ State/Prov. _____ Zip/Postal Code

* In Canada, mail to: Silhouette Canadian Book Club,
320 Steelcase Rd., E., Markham, Ontario, L3R 2M1, Canada
Terms and prices subject to change.
SILHOUETTE INTIMATE MOMENTS is a service mark and registered trademark.

Silhouette Desire

COMING NEXT MONTH

TANGLED WEB—Lass Small
The object of an outrageous matchmaking scheme, Peggy Dillon found herself at the mercy of a fat old dog, invisible alligators and a man determined to win her heart.

HAWK'S FLIGHT—Annette Broadrick
Dr. Paige Winston wasn't used to the rugged life, but when she found herself stranded in the Arizona mountains with handsome adventurer Hawk Cameron, she had to learn fast.

TAKEN BY STORM—Laurien Blair
Teenage-advice columnist Randy Wade thought she had all the answers, but when single parent Nick Jarros stormed into her office, she found herself at a loss for words.

BEWITCHED—Sara Chance
Isis O'Shea possessed an unusual talent, a talent that James Leland needed. Was his courtship of the beautiful psychic the beginning of love or just the means to an end?

A COLDHEARTED MAN—Lucy Gordon
Accused of a crime that she had no memory of committing, Helena knew her only defense rested in the hands of the man she loved…the man she'd jilted ten years before.

NAUGHTY, BUT NICE—Jo Ann Algermissen
Damon Foxx was one of the socially elite, and Tamara Smith was a "bad girl" from the wrong side of the tracks. Falling in love was definitely against the rules!

AVAILABLE NOW: